Designer Deceit

Bitches of Fifth Avenue
Book Three

Books by Toni Glickman

Bitches of Fifth Avenue
Book One: Champagne at Seven!
Book Two: Cutthroat Couture
Book Three: Designer Deceit

**For more information
visit:** www.SpeakingVolumes.us

Designer Deceit

Bitches of Fifth Avenue
Book Three

Toni Glickman

SPEAKING VOLUMES, LLC
NAPLES, FLORIDA
2025

Designer Deceit

Copyright © 2025 by Toni Glickman

All rights reserved. No part of this book may be reproduced or transmitted in any form or by any means without written permission.

This book is a work of fiction. All names, characters, places, and events are the product of the author's imagination. Any resemblance to actual events or persons, living or dead, is entirely coincidental.

ISBN 979-8-89022-201-5

Chapter One

"Mom, I know. Please!! Don't you think I understand the severity of what happened?" Olivia is still in shock and utterly exhausted from all of the drama. "And, where exactly did Gwynnie get this brazil nut?" asked Gladys. "Seriously? I have no idea, Mom! You think I'd want her to have had this acute anaphylactic allergic reaction? I'm guessing she got it at school! Maybe another kid had them and she tried one . . . all I care about is that she is ok. Could you please curb the extra and unnecessary drama?! All you do is hyperbolize. It's too much and I can't take it! Please be logical for one minute of your life." Olivia rushed to University Hospital as soon as she got the news. By then, Gwynnie was resting comfortably with an IV cocktail full of anti-anaphylactic meds: an epinephrine infusion, steroids, antihistamine and an antibiotic. "She clearly ate it not knowing she had this severe of an allergy! From here on out, we all carry Epi-Pens and have an extra as backup. I've cleaned out everything and anything nut oriented from the pantry and fridge—we are now an official nut-free zone!" Olivia takes a deep inhale and then exhales with closed eyes. "Ok, I'm really worn out and need to go to bed. My back is fucking killing me, and this headache is blinding." Olivia gets up from a kitchen stool and slowly starts to make her way to the stairs leading up to the bedroom. "Olivia, please, what was the doctor's name at the hospital? I'd like to call and thank him for taking such beautiful care of our Gwendolyn . . . my gorgeous granddaughter. Maybe I'll send a gift." Olivia, halfway up the stairs, turns towards the kitchen and says, "Are you really serious? I can't remember now . . . I'm too exhausted to think. And you are not sending a gift. Wait, hold on, maybe Feldman or Friedman or something. No idea of the first name. Only Dr. Whatever. I suppose you could call the nurse's desk and ask. Do you seriously need to know right now?" Gladys's eyes light up . . . "Ohhh! Jewish! Is he single? You need to think about getting out again, darling." Olivia chuckles, "Oh, please. Dating is the very last thing on my mind. And honestly Mom? Really?" Olivia rolls her eyes and thinks *give me a break.* Olivia drags herself up the stairs and grips the handrail for stability. *Holy shit I'm tired.* Closing the bedroom door behind her, Olivia drops onto the bed, closes her eyes, takes a deep, intensely long breath, and ploddingly and deliberately exhales this extra layer of theatrics. She changes into an oversized and ripped graphic tee and a pair of Gwynnie's sweats. Slumped over with exhaustion and with no blow dry to protect, she grabs her hair and pulls it all back with the simplest of black Goody hair bands resulting in a tangled mess on top of her head. Finally washing her makeup and the stress of the day off her face with a sample Skincando CBD cleansing oil & makeup remover, Olivia reads the label: *luxury organic skincare . . . one of the country's first green beauty brands . . .* She was saving it but thought no better time than the present for some seriously necessary self-care. Fortunately, she also had a sample of the brand's Miracle Cream . . . *scented with pure rose essential oil and handcrafted in micro batches . . .* A light application to finish her skincare sampled evening bedtime beauty routine sounded perfect. She remembers the days of full sized and full priced everything, shampoos, skincare, hand lotion and toothpaste. *Never mind*, she thinks. *A day at a time. I'll get there . . .* crawling into bed, Olivia counts the hours until she needs to get back to the Salon. *Ok, if I sleep right now, I'll have four hours . . . if I'm lucky. Quick wake up, shower, coffee and train into the city and then more coffee . . . ugh, I need sleep.* Olivia falls quickly into slumber, letting the day's stress and anxiety fade away. At least for now.

***

Entering the Salon the next morning, Olivia is still tired, though ready to take on the day. She is pulled together and can't wait to take on this client of Chrissy's. *This will be interesting,* she thinks. Still, something is up. *Why would Chrissy be so nice and offer me this client? Strange. Time will tell, I guess.* Olivia takes another sip of her Starbucks dark roast with extra cream.

Always trust your gut, thinks Olivia.

"I must tell you, Olivia, I find the juxtaposition fascinating," says Amby, observing the dress from every angle. "The ruffled neckline with the asymmetrical hem . . . it's very Little House on the Prairie meets Barbarella? Colonial mod, that's the term. Write that down, will you, Dominique?"

Dominique immediately reaches for her notepad, frantically jotting a note. "Got it!" she says. "I love that, Amby!"

Next to her, two handsome young men—The Boys, as Amby introduced them to her, nod simultaneously.

"Brilliant," says one.

"Sublime observation," says the other.

"I think that's very astute insight, Amby," says Olivia, feeling both relieved and on edge. She'd only had half an hour to pull the clothes, and had gone with her gut, choosing the best and most unique pieces she could find. Edgy, non-traditional, just a bit off with a definite cool factor.

Nothing, though, could be more off than this scene.

But one question remains. *Does she like it?* Olivia sucks in her breath, waiting.

"Hmmm," says Amby, observing herself through narrowed eyes. "Colonial Mod, that's the term. I oughta trademark that . . . make a note, Dominique."

***

After their agreement on the fire escape, Chrissy had perked right up, back to her old enthusiastic self. Only this time, it was minus the Olivia shade. "Oh my God, you are the best, Olivia!" She'd squealed. "I gotta get on this!"

Chrissy called Amby's assistant, explaining she had an emergency, but not to worry. "I've got the perfect fill in," she'd said. "She's awesome! She'll get Amby something perfect, you'll see!" She'd hung up and started a text to Olivia. "I can't thank you enough . . . I really can't. They say fine," she squealed while simultaneously writing the text.

Seconds later, Chrissy's phone had beeped.

"Zoe!" Chrissy had said. "I told her I made other arrangements for Amby, and she's not mad anymore! If I bust my ass, I can meet you guys just in time for the infrared LED light vaginal-tightening sauna treatment." When Zoe heard that her *arrangements* entailed Olivia, she was less than thrilled. But by that point, Chrissy was already in a frenzy, rushing to fix her makeup and meet the girls ASAP. "Well, Chrissy, let's just sit back and watch. I can't wait." Zoe rudely hung up on Chrissy as she usually did when she decided a call was finished.

***

Pulling clothes that morning involved racing throughout all departments of the store and enlisting the help of her counter girl allies, but somehow, Olivia and a rack made it back to the Salon just in time. Moments later, at 11:00 on the dot, Amby arrived.

She wasn't alone.

Amby appeared in a simple shift dress. Winter white, it was a stark contrast to the sea of black behind her. An entourage, all whippet thin and clad in harsh skintight leather and vinyl. They made quite an entrance, and Olivia could feel other personal shoppers turning to stare. "Oh my God," someone had whispered loudly, "That can't be . . ."

"Amby," said another voice, then gave an uncomfortable laugh. Olivia had turned around, shooting a glare at the commentators—Gia, who'd quickly looked away, and Ursula, staring right back with one arched eyebrow raised and a smugly defiant look on her face.

Olivia told herself to ignore them, instead focusing on the task at hand and directly in front of her. "You must be Amby," she said. "Such a pleasure! I hadn't expected you to bring friends, but . . ."

"Oh, them? They go where I go," said Amby. "And why don't you show us exactly where that is, hmmm?"

***

Now they were all crammed into a too-small space, watching as Amby models the first dress. Forty-five minutes into the appointment and Amby has rhapsodized on a variety of topics, taking her time with the process. It has taken all that time to get her into a dress, yet she seems more interested in discussing trademarking opportunities than offering a verdict on the very reason she is here—to shop.

"Colonial Mod!" gushes Dominique. "Genius!"

"It'll be bigger than Meth Head Chic," says one of The Boys.

"Bigger," agrees the other.

Besides Olivia, there's Amby and her assistant, Dominique. Next to her are The Boys—one is a manager, the other a publicist, though it is hard to tell who is who. And their titles seem pointless, Olivia has quickly realized—their true job is to smile, nod and agree with Amby's every sentiment. It doesn't matter the feeling, be it what is the most superior bottled water brand (*Evian of course. Hand me that bottle, will you, Dominique?*) to the ins and outs of fashion aesthetics (*I loathe color blocking and ribbons of all kinds. When it comes to a "frill," the only acceptable ones are just that. Necessary to the overall aesthetic commentary of the piece. So please abstain from showing me anything that does not meet these requirements!*)

To each observation, the same reaction. Some variation of *you're absolutely right, Amby.*

As for the final observer, Olivia has yet to learn the girl's name. Purple-haired, heavily pierced and silent, she stares out from beneath dark cat-eyed black kohl liner, watching everything with a curious expression.

Olivia watches Amby consider the Simone Rocha embellished frill dress—a necessary enhancement, Olivia hopes—and wonders what she's gotten herself into. She had expected the Amby from those early 2000's magazines, wild and free, getting into trouble and making unorthodox statements to the press. Or the Amby of her punk rock stage, posing in Courtney Love-esque rips with a fist in the air. Or even the international playgirl who has given up on America, choosing instead to jet set the world and take the occasional payout as a high-paid DJ. Or, if you believe the rumors, secretly work as an escort. Pictures surfaced once with her in a club and at a table seated right next to Matt Gaetz, but it was later proven that Amby only slightly knew someone else in the group and that she had no relation to the scandalous Congressman. Who really knows if those sex parties really happened and who would want to have sex with Gaetz anyway.

Only this Amby is unexpected—direct, every sentiment parlayed with direct seriousness. There was no giddiness, or sharp edge, and at first Olivia had chalked that up to exhaustion. She'd just come in the night before, Amby explained, and was terribly jet lagged. "Oh, were you somewhere fabulous?" Olivia had asked, expecting some elite tropic locale or champagne private super yacht party in Ibiza. "I heard you are an extraordinary DJ."

"I don't dedicate my talents to such petty pursuits anymore," Amby had said, giving Olivia a penetrating look. "I was at an Ashram in Hyderabad. The vomiting and diarrhea were non-stop. Do I look skinny?"

The most surprising part of it all? Amby's intelligence. Long ago dubbed a vapid party girl with unexpected business sense. "Dumb as a fox," people said.

Generally citing her strategic branding and large net worth, Amby was known for her naïveté and silly observations. But this Amby isn't frivolous or dismissible, and Olivia is finding her perspective well thought out. Only the first item of clothing, and every statement she's made has shown an astute understanding of fashion, both historically and in actual construction.

Only now, watching her contemplate the dress in silence, there is one more question.

"So," says Olivia. "What do you think?"

"I need a deeper perspective," says Amby, then turns to the silent, pierced girl. "Luna?" Immediately, the girl is on her feet, heading towards the platform. Everyone watches in heavy silence as she lifts her hands, holding them inches from the dress, and closes her eyes. A good minute passes. *What in the world?* thinks Olivia.

Suddenly, the girls' eyes pop open. She steps back with a beautiful smile, then gives a small nod.

Amby turns to Olivia. "This dress has good energy," she says.

"Good energy?" repeats Olivia. "That's great, I've just never heard of a dress having any sort of energy."

"Luna reads vibrations," says Amby, smiling for the first time. "She's an energy healer."

Luna raises her eyebrows.

"And a Reiki Master," Amby adds, still smiling at Luna. "She also dabbles in animal communication. She's famous for transmitting signals to ferrets and small rodents. In other words, she's pretty much an all-around genius." The two grin at each other, lost in their own energy universe.

If there's any healing going on here, Olivia thinks, *it's the sexual kind.*

Amby breaks the spell, turning abruptly to Olivia. "I'll take it," she says, then pauses, contemplating Olivia with narrowed eyes. "You're very good at this, you know. You understand my style."

At least I understand something, thinks Olivia. *Because I've officially entered Crazy town.*

"That's nice of you to say," responds Olivia. "It's always . . ."

"Yes, this will work out," she interrupts, turning away. "Does everyone agree?"

"You're absolutely right," says Dominique.

"Brilliant," announce The Boys.

To her left, Luna offers yet another nod.

"Good, then it's settled," says Amby. "Now show me what else you've got."

***

Three hours and thousands of dollars later, Olivia escorts Amby towards the Salon lobby. Close behind are Dominique and The Boys, loaded down with Harper James bags. Olivia said she could have everything delivered, but Amby just shook her head. "No, no," she responded. "I need to be with the clothes immediately. Especially the accessories. They need time to adjust to my realm, and I to theirs."

"Oh, of course. I understand." Chimed Olivia. By this point, she knew not to ask questions.

Olivia knows the audience; the whole Salon is watching in amazement. But they are the last thing she is thinking about.

Olivia nailed it. Seriously nailed it.

She took everything. The Alexander McQueen harness top, the Versace strapless tartan gold studded, leather-trimmed dress, the Fendi metallic glazed checked pants suit. The Carolina Herrera ballroom skirt and Tory Burch bell sleeved shift dress, all of the belts, shoes and bags, and . . . maybe it was divine inspiration, or simply sex appeal, but Luna nodded so much she looked like a bobble head.

Olivia, it seems, is exuding good energy.

Who cares if people are watching? Olivia thinks. The sale is so big, she can hardly fathom it, and she feels on top of the world. She did a favor, and look where it got her. Good energy, good karma . . . good selling skills. Whatever the reason, it is just the boost she needs before tomorrow.

At the Salon door, Amby stops suddenly. "I had my doubts about today, Olivia. I'm very picky when it comes to apparel, even more since my awakening."

Olivia knows not to ask.

"I hadn't wanted to come today, but Dominique insisted. Now I know the universe was pointing me in the right direction." She reaches out suddenly, clasping Olivia's hand in her own.

"You understand me," she says. "We have a connection. A real synergy."

Olivia isn't sure how to respond, but it doesn't matter. Just as quickly, Amby drops her hand. "Come along," she calls to her minions. "I'm dying for an Appalachian Mountain spring water-processed, decaf, organic Swiss almond milk, Vietnamese cinnamon mochaccino."

And, just like that, they are gone.

Olivia turns around, and everyone is suddenly busy, careful not to meet her eyes. Not that she expected a congratulations or gold medal or anything, but it seems extreme, treating her like a fashion leper after she just made the biggest sale she could possibly imagine.

That's when Ursula looks up from the rack she is sorting, catching Olivia's eyes.

See? Thinks Olivia, giving her a smile. *You didn't think I could do it, but I'm better than you thought, right?*

Ursula shakes her head, gives a little snort and turns away.

Fine, thinks Olivia. *Don't think I can do this? Watch me.*

***

It's the next morning already and Olivia is a bundle of nerves. At least Gwynnie is on the mend after that terrible brazil nut fiasco. "Mom, I swear I'm ok. Would you please get to work already!" Olivia looks at her watch, it's not the Cartier Ballon Bleu automatic rose gold diamond model she once had, though never mind, at least she had a watch. Though it was already on sale for $2.99 on Temu, the low-priced, get anything you want retail website. And . . . she thought the $6.99 she bought it for was a bargain.

The reporter is due at 10:00 a.m. Now, at 9:55, she is ready. Today's lipstick shade is a hot cherry rosette. Olivia reapplies, hands shaking. The shade is not her usual subtle pink, but much bolder. The deep rose of a woman in control; a woman who rules her own destiny.

The racks of clothes are finally ready. Her desk is spotless, as is she. True, the Salon environment is worse than ever—no one would acknowledge her that morning, not even C-Cup Chrissy. Not that she expected their relationship to have fast forwarded to BFF status, but just a thankful look or even a hello would have been enough. Instead, just like all the others, she'd gone to great lengths to avoid Olivia's eyes.

At least Zoe wasn't around. Small mercies.

Still, Olivia does not feel completely alone. She has supporters, albeit from afar.

***

Come to find out, as shocked as Olivia was by this turn of events, her family had been more overwhelmed when she came home that one night. Gwynnie had run over and hugged her, "That's so cool, Mom! That is seriously huge!" she'd said. "I knew you could do it! Eff the man, right?"

"Language," said Gladys.

"Eff the woman in this case. Women, I mean," Gwynnie had said, ignoring her. "Those catty Salon chicks didn't stand a chance . . . you got serious cred, Mom. *WSD?* That's beyond."

Gladys had been less enthusiastic. "I don't understand." "Are you sure they didn't make a mistake? Maybe you misunderstood what Felix was saying."

Olivia was on such a high, she wasn't even annoyed. She just explained again, and once Gladys understood her, the woman had been overcome. "Such a prestigious publication! But I'm not surprised, not at all. You have true style, Olivia. A real eye. Hmmm . . . wonder where you got that from?"

Olivia realized she had to share the amazing news with Daphne. After four rings, the voice mail came on. "Hello, lovey, beautiful rose petal. I'm so sorry I can't pick up your call right now. But please do leave me a detailed message and I promise to ring you back just as soon as possible. Thank you! Much love, darling!" *I hate voicemail,* Olivia thinks. *So impersonal.* "Daphne! It's me, Olivia. How are you? I miss you so much. I have some great news to share. You must call me. Ok, lots of love. Talk with you soon."

That morning, her mother insisted on overseeing her look for the day, okaying her wide-cut black wool pants and simple long-sleeved silk cream blouse. The look was anchored by a smart, but simple black leather belt with large silver Gucci G's. She looked chic yet understated—a real professional. But Gladys wasn't satisfied. "It's missing one thing," she said, disappearing into the depths of her closet and returning with a shoebox.

"Mom! I didn't know you had Louboutins!" Olivia had opened the box carefully, marveling at the classic black pumps, the red soles. They were in perfect condition—elegant, pristine.

"I bought them for you," Gladys had said.

"For me? When?"

"Years ago. We weren't speaking much then. It was when Edwin was at his asshole prime. But I couldn't help it. Olivia would look amazing in these, that's what I thought. The next moment, I was taking out my credit card." Gladys smiled. "I thought, one day I'll give them to her. One day she'll come back here, and I'll have the chance. I think now is as perfect a time as any."

***

And now it is happening. Happening in a mere three minutes.

She looks around the fitting room—everything is ready and in place. Now all that's missing is the final touch. Olivia pulls the tube from her purse and heads to the platform. She brings it to her lips, and with careful precision, turns the tube, watching the stick turn upwards. That bold color is a suit of armor, but also a flag to the world: she is unstoppable. Divert your eyes or glare, call her any name you want—think she is an imposter, a fraud or unworthy. She waits nervously among these other pitiful excuses of professionals. *True classless acts!* she thinks.

This rosy-lipped fashionista won't be hindered, that's what Olivia tells herself. But even at that moment, seeing three strong, capable women staring back from the three-way mirror, she admits the other part. Just beneath the rush of confidence, there are the little bubbles of fear. Like little bubbles moving upwards from a fresh pour of her favorite Robert Monquit, though, these days, more like bubbles from basic rail club soda.

A buzzer goes off. Olivia turns and closes the tube with a click.

Time to take center stage. Too bad it isn't Broadway.

***

Olivia is a half-second too late. Zoe has arrived—just stepped through the doorway, in fact, still wearing her coat. Next to her, someone else, seeming to have arrived simultaneously.

"Sorry, are you lost?" she says. "We weren't expecting a delivery."

False alarm? Still, Olivia speed walks over, just in case.

"Is this the Salon?"

That couldn't be . . .

"Yes," says Zoe. "Were you making a delivery? Those go to the mail room downstairs."

"Good to know," says the guy, then he grins. "But I'm here for another reason. Your name isn't Olivia, by chance?"

Oh fuck.

***

When it came to Blake Goldman, Olivia had expectations. In preparation for his visit, she spent the evening before googling his name, reading several of his pieces. As a political journalist, Blake had been sharp and savvy, wryly peeling away the layers of authority with insightful observations. His more recent venture in fashion journalism was equally enthralling, profiling major figures and brands with revealing detail that painted the industry as it really was—full of captivating personalities and genius, but also weakness. Theatrics. Still, even when pointing out greed or narcissism, he never made fun of the industry, or took away from its global societal influence. If anything, he seemed to honor the legacy above all. Olivia had been excited reading those pieces. *This guy will understand the Salon,* she'd thought, eager to put a face to the man.

Considering the details that he used in his pieces, and the highbrow turn of phrase, Olivia sensed an innate understanding of style. He'd be one of those well put-together types, she figured, imagining him to be conservative and sophisticated. In a recent profile of forthcoming trends, for example, he'd focused on textiles—specifically tapestry—offering historical context to modern connotations.

From adorning fifteenth century castles to your grandmother's kitchen wallpaper, the connotations range from elitist decadence to 1940's kitsch. Yet current designers have reimagined this textile into something entirely modern, meshing opulence, everyday utility and a dash of sex appeal. Once the domain of royalty, today's woman can embrace everyday opulence, cocooning herself in an Alexander McQueen coat adorned with woven butterflies on the average Tuesday. Forget the boredom of a life of leisure; whether hailing a taxi or picking up a carton of milk at the corner bodega, she is the epitome of a modern-day princess . . .

As for the man himself, in all her googling there had only been one photo—a classic off-the-cuff journalist shot, taken in profile. Taken outdoors with the sunset behind, he gazes off into the distance. His hair is windswept, his features just barely discernible. Not much to go on, but based on the writing itself, Olivia had formed a clearer image in her head.

A guy with Goldman's understanding of style, she figured, would be put together, sophisticated. Well-fitting, flat front pants, a button up shirt—maybe a cashmere sweater. She'd even pictured a scarf, knotted Scandinavian-style. If she were going to be honest, she assumed he'd be gay. Totally cliché, she knew, but gay men were prevalent in the industry. And few straight guys had such fashion insight, right? One might profile or assume. Olivia did her best not to do either.

***

"Olivia?" says Zoe, a catch in her voice. "You're looking for Olivia?"

Olivia had been wrong about pretty much everything. This guy doesn't exactly exude sophistication—in dark indigo slouchy jeans and slightly oversized navy polo shirt, he looks like he's headed to a sports bar. He's even wearing sneakers, and not the $900 kind either . . . the kind you get in a suburban outlet mall, not some hip Soho store. Stan Smith's to be exact. He's got wire-rim glasses. Hair slightly messy, and not in that purposeful way that you pay some overpriced stylist to create. 40? 45? Or maybe older even. He's vaguely cute, but in more of a former frat boy way than that of a high-level fashion commentator.

"You're not . . . are you from WSD?" says Zoe.

Step in, thinks Olivia. *Introduce yourself.* Yet, for some reason, she feels frozen in place, watching the action before her like a slow-motion, shit show train wreck.

He nods, and Zoe instantly goes into alert, standing up straighter. "Oh wow," she trills, voice lifting as she shifts into charm mode. "I'm so excited to meet you! We are thrilled you'll be covering the Salon," she says. "This place is magical. I'd be happy to tell you more if you have the time."

"So, you are Olivia Kopelman?"

"No," Olivia finally blurts, only the word is too loud, too harsh. Immediately, everyone turns to her. She takes a quick breath, composing herself, then gives a rosy smile. "That would be me," she says.

Blake strides over, Zoe immediately forgotten. "Hi," he says, extending a hand.

"You must be Blake Goldman," says Olivia, shaking his hand. "Sorry for the confusion. I'm Olivia."

They smile at each other, and Olivia tells herself to focus and not think of anything else. Especially Zoe, who is just beyond his left shoulder, glaring like a starving animal ready to tear into her flesh.

"Welcome to the Salon, Mr. Goldman."

"Blake."

"Blake. Shall we start with a tour?"

***

"So, this is Harper James's most iconic department?" says Blake. "Fancy place. Hey, mind if I tape this?"

"No problem," says Olivia, and watches him remove a small recorder from his pocket and press a button. "So, the Salon was introduced in Harper James's early years, and a great deal has remained the same. This is the original space, and as you probably know, it has hosted some of New York's most iconic personalities."

"You're like a human press release," says Blake, stopping Olivia cold.

"Um, no. I just thought I'd give you a little background."

"I have Google for that," he says. "I want to really know this place on a more intimate level, the daily details. Average scenarios. Clients. So be yourself."

"I always am, Blake," says Olivia.

"I'm sure . . . it's just reporters, right? People get uncomfortable. I just want a sense of the Salon as it really is, day to day."

"Sure," she says, motioning for him to follow. "So, as you can see, every employee has their own desk."

"How many personal shoppers are there?"

"Right now? Seven."

"High turnover rate?"

"Well, some are early in their careers while others are more established. More seasoned, if you will. One shopper, Glory, has been here for over a decade."

Blake nods. *Good job,* Olivia tells herself. *That was some straight-up White House press conference deflection.*

"So, you all have your own desks?"

"Exactly," she says. "For instance, this one belongs to Gia." In the corner, where she is sorting garments, Gia looks up, surprised. "Gia, this is Blake Goldman. The journalist from *WSD*."

In a matter of seconds, Gia goes from confusion to wariness. Not that Blake can tell any difference—you'd have to observe the guarded, emotionless woman silently from a hidden desk to pick up on the change, that's how subtle it is. But Olivia catches the flash in her eyes, and knows what it means– *are you messing with me? Is this a trick?*

It isn't about her really, it's about making the Salon look professional, creating an impression of grace and know-how. And Gia is an expert at that, immediately snapping into gear, sinking over with a bright smile. They chat for a moment, Gia explaining that her next client is model-turned-actress. "The talent agency wants to launch her with some public appearances, so they called me," she says. "I'm going for something hip, yet sophisticated." She motions to the rack. "I pulled some Isabel Marant dresses, a few Barbara Bui separates; skirts, slacks and elegant silk blouses."

"Is she?" asks Blake.

"Is she . . . what?"

"Hip and sophisticated?"

Gia raises her eyebrows. "She's whatever the agency wants her to be."

For a second, nobody knows what to say.

"How about I show you the back stock area?" asks Olivia. "Where we keep new merchandise and additional sizes of what's already on the selling floor. I mean, maybe that's not the kind of thing you want to see . . ."

"I want to see everything, Olivia." *Hmmm . . . see everything?* Olivia wonders and thinks, *they're all the same!*

"OK then, Follow me."

***

In the back hallway, Olivia leads him towards the stockroom at the end. As they go past Glory's hold closet, there is the sound of someone singing to themselves—off key and accompanied by a distinct aroma. It seems to be coming from . . .

Shit. She didn't know Glory was even here. And apparently, she's having the kind of breakfast you inhale.

"Wow," says Blake, inhaling. "What's going on behind Door #1?"

"Oh, that's one of our shoppers," says Olivia quickly, ushering him down the hallway. "Probably busy preparing for a client. You can meet her later."

"Got a feeling she's a lot of fun," he says, falling behind, smiling wryly.

"She's great," says Olivia, then quickly changes the subject. "We have a ton of rotating inventory, so we keep some in the back."

"I mean, WTF?" booms a voice. "It makes no sense."

It's coming from a little way down—the breakroom—loud, echoing and unmistakable.

"Like, who is that guy?" squeals Chrissy, aka Sorority Twin, aka one half of the dreaded C-Cups.

"Just follow me," Olivia says quickly, picking up speed. "Right this way."

"I mean, what kind of fashion journalist looks like that?"

Olivia cringes. She turns to see Blake Goldman is no longer following. He has stopped in the middle of the hallway, just a few feet from the breakroom. *Fuck,* thinks Olivia. *He's gonna be really . . .*

Only he's smiling. Olivia opens her mouth to speak, and he stops her with a finger to his lips. *I wanna hear this*, he mouths, still grinning.

"I don't know," says another voice. Catie. *She wouldn't dare*, thinks Olivia. *Not after I had her back with Amby.* "I think he's kinda cute. You know, in that East Village artsy way."

Blake raises his eyebrows at Olivia. *Cute*, he mouths, pointing to himself, still smiling, with a hint of flush.

Okay, that wasn't so bad, Olivia thinks, almost laughing.

Still, she's got to get him out of here. She backtracks towards him, brain spinning with *what the hell to do now*. When she's next to him, she gives an embarrassed smile. "Fashion types, you know," she says quietly. "Perhaps we should just press on?"

"If you like that type, I suppose," says a high-pitched voice.

Shit, not fast enough. This time, the voice is unmistakable—lilting, lighter than air. "But for an industry professional?" Zoe continues. "It is shocking, really. I mean, he works in fashion, and he was wearing those nasty sneakers? I mean who is Stan Smith? And those jeans? Disgusting!"

There are giggles.

"I know," pipes in Chrissy. "Those jeans! If they were Italian, maybe. But those were just like old nasty 1970's Levis or something."

"Who is he, exactly?" interrupts Zoe. "What are his credentials? This guy is not qualified to cover luxury retail, that's for sure. Uniqlo on a good day. Maybe."

From inside the Salon, a buzzer sounds. Olivia's appointment.

"That's my eleven o'clock," says Olivia with quiet intensity. "Time to go."

Blake, still grinning, motions towards the reception. He raises his eyebrows, as if to say, *'What are you waiting for, then? After you.'*

***

Walking towards the Salon's foyer, Olivia gives an apologetic smile. "I don't even know what to say."

"Don't worry about it," Blake says, still wearing a slight grin. "They aren't Italian, but indeed vintage 501's. The kind James Dean wore. They at least somehow got that right." He winks. "Kids today have no appreciation for the classics, Olivia."

Olivia can't help but laugh.

"Who cares either way? I just *write* about fashion. Now where is this client of yours? It's time to see what a real professional can do."

"Are you Mrs. Gladstone?" asks Olivia, greeting the elegant woman in the waiting room.

"You are Olivia, I take it." Olivia nods, and the woman turns to Blake. "And you must be the journalist I've heard about. I would never agree to this little escapade, except Felix vouched for you. I am not overtly trustworthy of those in the field, but Felix raved about the caliber of your writing. Though my husband does enjoy going head-to-head with the press!"

She need not say more.

"Wait, you're Melinda Gladstone?" asked Blake, taken aback. "I've been following your husband's endeavors for years."

"You and everyone else in the tri-state area," she says, then turns to Olivia and demands, "Let's get started, then. Come on Olivia. It's time to impress me with your innate and incredible styling skills."

* * *

When Olivia read Felix's email rundown of her first client, the name immediately jumped out at her. Everyone knew of the Gladstones—but the surprise had been exactly which Gladstone.

Melinda needs an evening dress for an upcoming fundraiser, Felix had written, *hosted by her husband, Ross.*

Ross Gladstone. Olivia knew who he was right away, as did most everyone in New York. An authentic blue blood with Mayflower roots, Ross was a notorious iconoclast, known for a fearless outspokenness, especially given his legacy. Ross was from a long line of the monetarily blessed—*where had it first come from, the money? Coal? Real estate? Shipping? Manufacturing? The name and assets were so established, it had ceased to matter, really*—he defied convention. While most Gladstone heirs engaged in lives of leisure, letting their investments grow, or slapping their name on a corporation, Ross was a real entrepreneur. Instead of sitting on his massive inheritance, he invested in a restaurant chain a decade earlier. "Who needs another 21 Club type place?" He'd told the press at the time. "Too bad it didn't make it; Covid was no friend to restaurants. But, regardless, it was overpriced and pretentious. Just give me a chicken burrito any day, extra guac and sour cream on the side."

While not exactly aligning with his upper-crust bloodline, the endeavor proved successful—by now, Gladstone Burrito Bars were all over the city. Cheap and delicious, they were the Tex-Mex themed equivalent to Starbucks.

Olivia had always admired the guy, both for his business savvy and fearlessness. He gave back, too, as did the entire Gladstone empire. But unlike previous generations, who shunned charitable works that involved actual people, Ross wasn't interested in having a plaque with his name graced on some antiquated building. Instead, he funded unexpected ventures—a hip-hop arts organization for rural children, a liberal candidate with not so thinly veiled socialist leanings. An independent LBGTQ bookstore, exotic faux skinned animal shelters, cutting edge kinetic energy powered environmental endeavors. Rumor had it that he palled around with similar renegades, socializing with the likes of De Niro and Woody Harrelson. Even Bernie Sanders and Greta Thunberg on occasion.

These were just some of the things Olivia had learned the night before during her Google search. Unfortunately, in all the press, there was little about Ross's wife, Melinda. Thirty-something and tall, with raven hair and refined features, she rarely made public statements.

As for her fashion sense, from what Olivia could gather, it leaned towards understated, uptown ready-to-wear. No bright colors, no unnecessary embellishments, no excess skin. Her choices were often described as refined and sophisticated by the press; Olivia saw them entirely differently. In her eyes, Melinda was a smoking hot MILF hidden behind layers of *boring*.

Maybe I can reform her wardrobe a bit, Olivia told herself. No big shake-ups, of course, as that would be too risky. *Perhaps a dash of flash, a pinch of color. An interesting detail at least. Shit, an opera-length necklace wrapped and styled in a way that would add a sense of chic, not shock.*

Olivia was forgiving of any fashion faux pas. She understood that not everyone instinctively knew how to dress and accessorize. One thing she could never forgive was *boring*. Existing without something memorable? Even a memorable shade of lipstick or nail polish. A pin. Some earrings, hair accessory, cool belt buckle. But nothing interesting? Forgettable everything? No, no, no and never allowed.

***

"It's a bit much, I think. With all that, you know, it's too frou frou."

"The embellishment? Once you put it on, you'll see it's rather subtle. And the silhouette will be gorgeous on you!"

"But the neckline . . . isn't it a bit, I don't know . . . overly provocative?"

Olivia glances at the charcoal gray Badgley Mischka gown she is holding—the neckline is far from plunging, and there is nothing frou-frou about it; intricate and unobtrusive, just giving the slightest hint of glimmer.

"I couldn't pull that off," says Melinda. "It's way too much."

This is the fifth suggestion with the same outcome. From the silk Stella McCartney to the overlaid Monique l'Huiller, each option has been high-end and undeniably elegant. Small embellishments, lace accents, a slightly lower back than her usual suit of armor silhouette—sure, they offer a tad more *oomph* than Melinda usually wears, but there is nothing extreme in the slightest.

At first, Olivia hadn't been too far off by Melinda's rejection. By dress three, she was still holding out hope, countering her silly arguments by pointing out all the attributes of the garment. *I need to make her see how beautiful she is,* Olivia kept thinking.

Olivia had been so engaged in the process she'd almost entirely forgotten about Blake. Then again, he had a way of disappearing, watching from a stool, hidden in the corner of the room, he seemed to blend into the space like a chameleon.

"I'm sorry, Olivia. It's just not my style."

Only now, with the rejection of dress four, the reality has set in. This is not working, not at all, and suddenly she's more aware of Blake than anything. Having a woman like Melinda Gladstone as a client was a huge deal, Olivia knew that. Felix probably went to great lengths to secure her visit, hoping to show the high-level of clientele the Salon keeps. But instead of excited squeals or gushing, all she's gotten is head shakes and the phrase *too much and I don't like it.*

What am I doing? If Olivia were smart, she'd just give the woman what she was used to—matronly, high-end ho-hum. There are countless boring dresses to pick from, even some of the more elite couture selections. But Olivia had to reinvent the wheel, didn't she? She had to get *clever*.

That's when Olivia realizes.

"Why are you hiding, Melinda?" The words just pop out of Olivia's mouth. *Oh shit.*

Melinda looks taken aback. "I'm not hiding anything."

"That's not what I meant. Hiding . . . yourself. Does that make sense?"

"No." The word is curt, yet there is curiosity in her eyes.

"Well, you are absolutely gorgeous. I'm sure you know that."

"I'm okay," she says. "But thank you."

"Yet, you go to these events, and . . . in all the photographs I've seen, your dresses are, well . . . understated. Sophisticated, sure, but . . . nothing that shows you off."

"My husband does enough of that for both of us."

"But what about you? Aren't you allowed to shine too?"

Melinda pauses, considering the question. "What would be the point?"

"Feeling beautiful. Admired."

"Admired?" Melinda gives a bitter laugh. "I know what they say about me, Olivia. Why would I want to draw more attention to that?"

"Say about you? I don't understand. I wasn't aware anyone was saying anything at all?"

"The people who attend those events," she cuts in. "The bigwigs and donors. My husband's family. And they are just echoing what's already out there. What the press puts out there." Melinda walks to a nearby chair and sits with a sigh.

"What stuff are you talking about?"

"C'mon, Olivia, really? I wish people would just tell the truth. When you're rich, they stop telling you what is real, it's the craziest thing. You can pay people to tell you the world is exactly how you want it to be."

Olivia nods. She is well-aware of the phenomenon.

"I know what people think . . . what they say. That I'm white trash, that I worked as an escort. That I'm a gold-digger, an airhead. A trophy wife."

Olivia is surprised. Sure, she ran across speculation about Melinda, but that was from years ago, and mainly originating from trashy gossip sites. In recent days, there is little beyond brief mentions in profiles of Ross, or captions in the society pages.

"Honestly, Melinda. That isn't out there. I just did a Google search on you last night." Olivia feels strange, admitting this. "I do it for all of my new clients, to get a sense of them. With you, that was difficult. I mean, maybe there was speculation from years ago, but . . . nothing recent. You are a clean slate."

"Please," she says, then looks across the studio. "Ask him. He knows."

Oh shit. She bites her lip, then turns. "Blake," she says, giving him a pointed look. "This is all off the record, right?"

"Of course," he says. "I turned off the tape recorder a while back."

"So, tell us. What do they say about Melinda in the press?"

"That she's beautiful. That she's married to a powerful man." He looks directly at her. "And that you are a complete mystery."

Melinda sits up straighter. "That can't be."

"It is," he says. "It's my job to know what's going on. I think people were curious years ago, when you first married. But that was, what? A decade ago?"

"Fifteen years."

Blake nods. "Since then, there's been nothing out there. Nothing I've seen. And I read a lot of press, trust me. I haven't seen any speculation, no rumors. Please, don't take this the wrong way, Melinda . . . but most people think of you as . . . *Ross Gladstone's wife*."

Olivia nods. "That's exactly what I meant," says Olivia. "So, what you intended came to fruition, Melinda."

"What do you mean?"

"You did exactly as you intended. You disappeared in plain sight."

Melinda shakes her head. "It sounds silly when you put it that way. But I suppose there's . . . some truth to it." Suddenly, her face crumples. A sudden tear streams down her cheek, *oh my God*, thinks Olivia. *I made my client cry . . . in front of a damn journalist, nonetheless.*

"I'm so sorry," says Olivia, grabbing a box of Kleenex and racing over. "Oh, Melinda, I didn't mean . . ."

"No, it's okay," she says, dabbing her eyes. "It's just . . . that's what Ross tells me all the time. *Why do you care what anyone thinks?* He once asked why I don't wear colors anymore, at least when we go out. But he doesn't get it, you know? He thinks I'm perfect. That I should be proud to show off." She shakes her head. "I can't believe I'm telling you all this, and in front of Blake even! But Felix said you'd understand me. He's a friend, you see, and has been telling me I need a fashion upgrade for, well . . . forever. Finally, I agreed. He really put on the pressure this time." She shakes her head. "So. I'm here." Melinda pauses, takes a deep breath, and then exhales slowly as tears stream down her face. "Why am

I crying?" She asks, as she dabs the corners of her eyes with tissue.

"You aren't out of the ordinary in that," says Olivia softly. "It's emotional sometimes, this process. It isn't just clothing, it's how we present ourselves to the world. A reflection of how we see ourselves inside."

"I didn't always see myself as . . . I don't know. Covered up and, how did you put it? Disappearing in plain sight. That wasn't how I was when I first met Ross. I'd try any trend." She smiles, remembering. "You wouldn't believe this, Olivia, but I always loved fashion growing up. The more glitz the better." She grins. "In fact, one year I was the Sedgwick County Wheat Queen. My evening wear dress was head to toe lemon yellow rhinestones," she says, then with a twang, "And a matching lemon-yellow rhinestone cowboy hat!"

"Are you from the south?"

"The midwest." she says, giggling. "Wichita, Kansas. So, there ya go . . . that's one rumor they got right. Not white trash, exactly, but I come from everyday folks. Then I moved to New York to be a model, fell in love with this rich, powerful man . . . and suddenly everyone was always judging. I didn't hide my background, exactly, I just didn't talk about it."

"Took on a different role. To protect yourself."

"Exactly. Down to the costume, even. Soon as I got married, I threw away everything in my wardrobe, then filled it with expensive, boring shit. Nothing exciting, true, but at least I wasn't giving them anything to talk about."

Olivia nods, understanding. She married a powerful man too and was thrust into a world whose rules didn't make sense. It took years of missteps and questioning to understand what was expected, and then a total reinvention to fit in. But after all that, the part never quite fit her, the costume never felt exactly right.

"That was a long time ago."

"Fifteen years."

"Maybe a few people called you a trophy wife in the beginning, but not anymore. After a decade, you have officially surpassed that title. But I will say, judging by how Ross looks at you in pictures, to him you will eternally shine. Just like those lemon-yellow rhinestones."

"That's so cheesy," says Melinda. "But sweet."

They smile at each other for a moment.

"You're no one's trophy, Melinda. But you're no wallflower, either. You've got to dress for who you really are."

"I'm not sure who that is anymore," says Melinda. She stands, then nods towards the dress rack. "So . . .

I'm not promising anything, okay? But guess we better get started if there's even the smallest chance."

"Smallest chance?"

"That we figure it out."

***

"That was impressive," says Blake. Olivia had just returned to her desk after ringing up Melinda's purchase and escorting her out. He is waiting, still perched on his stool in the corner. "It was a large sale, right?"

Straightening the racks, her back to Blake, Olivia allows herself a huge smile.

"Let me put it this way," says Olivia, "It was more than adequate."

"Hence the smile. I can see your reflection in the mirror."

So much for playing it cool. Still, Olivia can't help but laugh. And the sale was definitely more than adequate, defying the odds in more ways than one.

"I've never observed a styling session," says Blake. "It was more emotional than I expected. The psychological element, I mean."

"They aren't all like that. But it happens sometimes. How a woman dresses reflects who she is or who she wants to become. How she feels about herself. So, all those insecurities, that confusion; the client can become vulnerable during an appointment and those feelings occasionally rise to the surface."

"Funny how an item of clothing can have that much power," says Blake, turning on his recorder again. "How it can change your entire perspective." Olivia suddenly thinks of the Chanel 2.55's—the ones she'd imagined would make her happy. Make her life complete. Then she pictures herself hiding them away in the closet, like a secret shame.

"Or not. It ultimately comes down to how you feel about yourself. Melinda is beautiful and charming and engaging . . . she'd just forgotten that at some point. In her case, the dresses were a physical manifestation of who she really is inside." Olivia pushes the rolling rack with the remaining dresses towards the wall. "You're sure you're not a part time psychologist?" asks Blake. "I mean, honestly, I couldn't find a thing about you online."

Olivia feels her pulse quicken. She cringes. Thank God she is turned away from him. "Oh, no?" she says lightly. "Well, I keep a low profile, I guess."

"When did you discover fashion?" Keep it together, thinks Olivia, forcing her face into a neutral mask. Keep calm. "Was it in college or later?"

". . . way earlier than that," says Olivia, turning around with a small smile. "I grew up in the apparel industry. My dad was a fabric manufacturer."

"So, fashion came naturally to you."

"Yeah," says Olivia. "But you were a political writer before, right?"

"I was."

"But you moved to fashion," she says. "That's a big change."

"How did you . . ."

"I can use Google, too."

Blake shakes his head, then glances at the recorder. "Hey, when did this turn into an interview about me?"

Olivia shrugs. "Just curious."

"Here's what I'm curious about . . ."

"Nice pivot."

"It's my gift." He grins. "So, I know you're relatively new to Harper James. In your time here, have you found the transition difficult?"

"So far, my clients have been great," says Olivia, her pulse once again speeding up.

"I'm sure. I meant the atmosphere. Here in the Salon."

"The atmosphere? I've been so busy I haven't noticed," she says, and Blake nods. He isn't quite satisfied with the answer, she can tell. "No, it is really busy here," she says lightly. "I'm either seeing a client or preparing for one, both of which take enormous effort. And luckily, so far, my clients seem pretty satisfied."

"I was curious about the camaraderie within the Salon," he pushes. "You're great at this work, no doubt. But . . ."

"But that's the point," says Olivia. "The focus of this job is the clients, not my colleagues, and so far, my clientele has been very happy with everything."

"Olivia?" says a voice. They look up to see Gia at the door.

Saved.

"We have an issue," she says.

Spoke too soon.

"An issue?"

"With a client," says Gia, mouth slightly downturned. "She's waiting out there for you."

Shit, thinks Olivia, glancing over to Blake. "I'll be right back," she says, but he's already standing.

"I'm supposed to trail you all day," he says. "But don't worry, you'll hardly notice me at all."

Olivia wants to argue, but one look at Gia stops her cold. She refuses to look weak in front of a co-worker. *Again.*

"Fine," she says, then heads towards the Salon foyer, the heaviness in her stomach like having had way too much pizza on Super Bowl Sunday.

A young woman in head-to-toe gold lame stands in the center of the Salon, surrounded by stuffed Harper James bags. "She hates it," she announces before Olivia has even crossed the room.

"I'm sorry," says Olivia, rushing over. "Have we . . ."

"I'm Dominique, Amby's assistant," she says, glancing down. "Sorry. You saw me on black day. Tuesdays are gold." Unlike the pliant, eager Dominique of yesterday, this version rolls her eyes and sighs. "Amby is a total freak, if you couldn't figure that out on your own."

"Wait, I don't understand," says Olivia, glancing down at all of the crinkled bags. She reaches inside one, pulling out several items—a Fendi dress, a Derek Lamb coat—thousands of dollars in couture that have been balled up and shoved haphazardly inside. "This looks pretty much like everything she bought?"

"Everything, yes. She wants to return it all."

"I don't understand," says Olivia, pulling out a pair of crumpled white silk Givenchy pants. "Oh my God," she says, dropping them just as quickly. "Was that blood? Oh my God."

"Yeah, sorry about that. Amby got her period. Yesterday wasn't so great. Even worse than usual. Really, really bad! Next level insanity for sure."

"Enough . . . I get it! But these pants have been worn. And stained with blood!"

"I don't know . . . maybe," says Dominique. "She said return them for a full refund."

"But . . . that's all she said?"

"Ummm, kinda." Dominique gives another sigh. "Oh, and that the Harper James Salon was a disappointment. She used other words, but that was the gist. A disappointment and she should never have taken the risk of going to a new place."

"Risk? But she comes here all the time, right?"

"Here? No. Someone called and pitched you guys, and Amby figured she'd give it a try. It was totally last minute, but she said it was a sign from the universe. She had just been going on about hating every outfit she owns. And she hasn't had luck anywhere else, and this friend of a friend or whatever said you were really great."

"Me?"

"Whomever. It doesn't matter." *Wait a minute,* thinks Olivia. She spins around, scans the room and spots them immediately. Zoe and Chrissy, pretending to discuss options on a rack, though they are really watching her. The second she spots them, they look away, but not fast enough. Olivia saw the amusement, the satisfied grins.

"I'm sorry, okay?" says Dominique. "It always ends up like this. Every single time." Olivia looks up to see Dominique inching away to the Salon door, leaving Olivia standing alone amidst the stuffed bags of balled up clothes. "Just credit her black card, and I promise we won't bother you again."

Before Olivia can respond, Dominique opens the door and slips out.

What the fuck?

Without thinking, Olivia turns on her heels, marching towards the girls. "Excuse me?" she says. Zoe takes a second before she looks up. "Are you okay?" she asks, eyes wide with innocent sympathy, her voice lighter than air.

"Tell me . . . where is Catie?"

"Catie?"

"You heard me. Is she hiding or something? I need to talk to her right now."

"Are you looking for me?"

There is Chrissy, magically appearing from behind the platform, her usual green juice in hand. She gives Olivia a glowing smile, looking quite the opposite of the broken, tear-streaked girl on the fire escape yesterday.

"Amby is your client, right?" says Olivia, making sure to keep her voice low.

"Yes, in a manner of speaking," says Chrissy, taking a slurp from her drink.

"A manner of . . . what does that mean?" hisses Olivia. "Look, have you styled her or not?"

"Well, I was supposed to yesterday," says Chrissy, then grins. "Then you were kind enough to take the appointment for me."

"Oh wait. You are talking about Amber Timberly?" asks Zoe.

"That's exactly whom I'm talking about."

"You didn't have an appointment with Amber Timberly, did you?" Olivia glares at her.

"You know perfectly well that . . ."

"Oh no, I guess you did," sighs Zoe, giving her a look of pity. "She came, bought a ton, and returned it, right? That's her thing. Banned from every personal shopping department in town." Zoe gives an innocent shrug. "I guess no one told you, huh?"

Stunned, Olivia looks at Chrissy who smiles, takes another obnoxiously loud green slurp and shrugs. Instantly, Olivia's shock transforms to fury—it pulses inside her like an equatorial heat wave, rising from her toes to her face. She will hurt this girl. She will reach out and smack her so hard green liquid will shoot out from her eyeballs.

"It's a shame that happened," says Zoe, her voice now barely a whisper. She glances over Olivia's shoulder. "Especially on such an important day."

Oh fuck, thinks Olivia, the hot fury turning ice cold. *Oh no . . .*

She turns, and there he is. Twenty feet away, watching the whole exchange with curiosity.

Get it together, Olivia.

She takes a deep breath, turning towards Blake with an apologetic smile. She walks calmly over to him.

"Listen, Blake . . ."

"Time for a treat, girls! Grab your coats," interrupts Zoe from behind her. "We're lunching! I made a rezzie at Nobu. Let's go."

A sudden burst of squealing. and Olivia forces herself not to cringe.

"It was great having you come by today. But . . ."

"Hey, don't say another word," he interrupts. "I know you're busy, and I got plenty of great stuff."

"I'm glad," says Olivia. To her left, Zoe and the C's head for the door, laughing as they discuss the calorie count of edamame. *Of course, they're leaving*, she thinks. *Not even giving me the chance to really call them out*. "If you have any more questions, I'm available," says Olivia.

A bang at the door slams behind them. Olivia does not jump or even look up.

"Just call or shoot me an email. I gave you my card, right?"

Blake nods. "But even better, I'd like to come back."

For a second, Olivia does not know what to say. "If you feel it will help the article," she finally manages.

"The more information the better," says Blake, putting on his coat.

"Well, I suppose that can be worked out."

"Great, then tomorrow?"

"I . . . need to check my schedule," says Olivia, already picturing the blank page in her head.

"How about we set a tentative time," says Blake. *Oh my God, this guy just won't let up.* "Two?" He reaches into his bag and holds out a card. "We can confirm in the morning. Just text, email . . . whatever works for you."

"Okay, sounds good!" says Olivia.

"Excellent," he says, already headed for the door. "I got a feeling, Olivia, there's a bigger story here to tell."

***

After Blake exits, Olivia stands there for a moment, trying to get a handle on herself. She wants to run for her junior fitting room in embarrassment and shame, but she won't let herself. She wants to stamp her feet and start yelling.

She knows that she is being watched. They are right behind her, just waiting for the reaction. Waiting to see what she will do next. Slowly, she counts backwards from five. Then with swift, emotionless precision, she turns and collects the bags of rumpled clothing.

God, everyone is just staring, she thinks. Watching her struggle with the clothes, not offering to help. Not saying a word.

"You should put Oxi-Clean on that stain," says Gia. "We have some in the breakroom."

"Thanks!" says Olivia, grateful for the distraction. Grateful for the acknowledgment, for something to do. Something other than standing there, being an object of pity and shame. "I'll do that!" she pipes up, sounding too cheerful, her voice strained.

She isn't thinking clearly, she knows that. That stain is set.

With as much grace as is humanly possible, Olivia loads a bag on each shoulder, the others, on her arms—too much to carry in one trip, she knows, but she does not intend to do this again. Loaded up, she slowly pulls herself to standing—steady, she tells herself, steady—until she has gotten her balance. She quickly walks towards the hallway, loaded down with those iconic, Harper James bags . . . only now packed with crumpled couture. She winces at the bag's black raffia handles cutting into her flesh.

Only once she is in the empty breakroom does she throw the bags off, groan, and lift a red welt-covered arm to her eyes. Only then, when no one can see her, does she allow the silent tears to come.

Oxi-Clean, she thinks frantically, racing to the counter. There it is. She grabs the pants, runs to the sink and pours it right on the red blotch.

So gross. All of it! The stain, this place. Zoe, the C's . . . in front of Blake, too! A fucking set-up, this whole thing.

Everything had been going so well! She'd won over Melinda, a tough client, an even bigger feat with Blake there. And Blakes's interview had gone well. She'd been authentic, yet collected, revealing, yet not giving away too much. He'd been impressed with her, she could tell. She'd made the Salon look good all while doing Felix proud.

Then, in an instant, everything changed. From triumph to shitshow in thirty seconds flat.

Suddenly she's pacing, unable to hold back the tears. Pacing the empty breakroom, crying, the wet ruined pants hanging limply from her hands. A barrage of images bearing down on her, one after the other.

Chrissy, on the fire escape, tear-streaked and pleading for help. *You are the only one I'd trust to do this, it just never occurred to me to ask.* Olivia agreeing and lunging in for a hug.

Amby clasping Olivia's hand. *You understand me. We have a connection.* Behind her, the entourage, loaded down with sparkling new ready-to-wear.

Little Dominique, in head-to-toe gold, loaded down with those same garments, now crumpled and squashed, the white silk pants stained from that female time of the month residual. *I bet that wasn't even an accident,* Olivia wonders.

Right then, it all becomes clear. Exactly who called to pitch Amby, and the expected result. They worked fast. Gotten that memo from HR and jumped into action. Less than an hour, but they were good. Maniacally good. Chrissy, drumming up those fake tears . . . she should have been a fucking actress, that one. But even worse, Zoe . . . Zoe, moments earlier, with her faux sympathy. Saying, *you didn't have an appointment with Amber Timberly, right?*

Banned. From every personal shopping department in town.

A fucking set-up. Olivia should have known.

Fuck! Her teeth clenched; Olivia throws the silk pants across the room. They smack against the wall, making a wet trail as they fall to the floor. It felt good, that throw . . . Olivia doesn't think, she just moves. Fury boiling up, she kicks, the point of her loaner Louboutin piercing into one of the crumpled bags. The contents fly upwards, and it feels amazing! She kicks another, even harder, then grabs a third and throws the contents up into the air.

She stops suddenly, watching the fabrics billow and fall. A rainbow rainfall of couture, and she, at the center is frozen in place.

OMG, w*hat is she doing?*

This place *is* Crazytown, an asylum of sorts and she's turning into a patient herself. This is what they want, exactly this . . . If she doesn't get out of here soon, she might do something drastic.

Panicked for breath, she quickly gathers the strewn items, shoving them all back into the bags. Shoving Chanel, Fendi and Givenchy into crumpled balls—that's how bad it's gotten. *Get out of here now*, she thinks, heaving them on her swollen and reddened arms. *Get the fuck out of here.*

That's what she does, speed walking through the door. Down the hallway, through the Salon . . . she doesn't look up, eyes focused straight ahead. *Get out of here now, before you do something you'll really regret . . .*

She's halfway to the elevator when a voice stops her cold.

"Olivia! Hold on!"

Oh God, what now? Olivia marched through the Salon, avoiding all eye contact, and made it to the hall.

"Olivia, just a second . . ."

Keep walking. Don't turn.

"Olivia, please . . . I'm too old to keep up . . ."

What now? Annoyed, she swings around to see . . . Glory, back against the wall. Leaned over, with hands to knees, huffing for breath.

Shit. Olivia races over.

"Are you okay?" she asks. "Do you need . . ."

"More exercise?" asks Glory. "Obviously. No, it isn't a heart attack."

"Are you sure?"

"Yes, I'm fine," she says, slowly rising upwards. "I was racing to catch up, and . . . didn't you hear me calling?"

Olivia sighs. "Not really. I just need to get the hell out of here."

Glory nods. "It was pretty shitty, what those girls did." Olivia stares at her. "Yes, I know. What I did was shitty, too. I'm so sorry about that, Olivia."

"Look, I'm really not up for some other pathetic showdown."

"I think about it all the time. That if I had stuck by you, perhaps. . ."

"I've got to get out of here," says Olivia firmly. "Wrong time and place, Glory. Not now. Not today."

"I know," says Glory. "I understand. I just wish I could make it up to you."

"You can't," says Olivia "It's too late."

Glory gives a sad nod. She looks so weary and exhausted Olivia feels her anger dissipate. "Look, it's fine now, okay? You did what you felt you had to. Maybe it wasn't . . . the kindest choice. You were protecting yourself, and now I have a better understanding of the big picture." Olivia forces a small smile. "I forgive you, okay? Consider this a truce. Now, I really have got to go."

"Thank you, Olivia."

Olivia nods and heads for the elevator. Only a few steps and she stops and turns around again. "Are you serious about making it up to me?"

"I am!"

"Well, I just might have a way."

Designer Deceit

***

Minutes later and only once she is out on the street does Olivia realize what she's carrying. Her arms are heavy with Amby's returned bags. *OMG what am I going to do with all of this? I didn't even realize what the hell I was doing or that I was still holding these bags. Holy shit!* Olivia takes the overflowing bags and opens the door leading back into Harper James. She quickly and quietly takes the seemingly endless number of Harper James shopping bags down the small flight of stairs, shuffles across the room through accessories, costume and fine jewelry, and swiftly lines them all up against the wall across from cosmetics. *I really don't care if that shit catches on fire.* She bolts out of the store exactly the way she just came in, not looking back or around despite the whispers and stares and turning heads all around her.

Lightheaded and with a sudden blinding headache, Olivia stands back out on the street, grabbing her cell phone and dials. Gladys picks up on the first ring.

"Mom?" she says, letting the tears fall freely. "This place is horrible! They're vultures . . . bitches! I'm really spent and cannot deal with the train right now. Please, can you come pick me up?"

Chapter Two

"Oh my God," says Gwynnie when Olivia enters the kitchen. "It didn't go well with the reporter, did it?"

"No, it went fine!" says Olivia, forcing a fake smile. Gwynnie narrows her eyes.

"So why did you call Granny crying? Why'd she race all the way into the city to pick you up? I was worried, Mom."

Olivia just sighs.

"What happened?"

"Give your mother a second, Gwynnie," says Gladys, who has already heard the whole thing. They had ridden in silence for a while, Gladys letting Olivia cry while periodically reaching over to grasp her daughter's hand. Only once they reached the bridge to New Jersey did the story finally come out. In bits and pieces, with tiny sobs between, but by the time they'd reached home, Gladys knew it all.

Now Gwynnie wants to know, too.

"Fine, just tell me this . . . those girls," says Gwynnie. "They tried to sabotage you, didn't they?"

"Gwyn, I said give your mother a moment to sit down."

"It's okay, Mom," says Olivia. "Yes, Gwynnie, they tried to. And they did."

***

In the hallway, Glory said she wanted to make things right, and Olivia gave her a way. *Get me a client*, she said. *By tomorrow morning.*

It was a risk, Olivia knew that. This was an emergency, with the store reputation at stake. She could just call Felix, or even Marguerite—they would help. But then they'd want to know what had happened, and Olivia couldn't trust herself to hold back after today.

After Felix had put so much trust in her, she'd have to admit she just wasn't up to the task. Sure, it was Zoe and the C's who had screwed her, but that didn't make it any better. A professional wouldn't have let that happen and admitting herself a failure to Felix or Marguerite filled her with dread.

Glory better fucking deliver.

A client? For tomorrow? Oh, that's rather last minute, Glory had responded, masterfully, stating the obvious.

"Never mind," Olivia had said, turning for the elevators. "Forget I said anything."

"I'll get you one, Olivia. I promise. I'll get you a client for tomorrow, and then we'll be even, right? You'll forgive me, and bygones will finally be bygones."

"Sure. But why does it matter to you so much?"

"I want to be right with the universe," Glory said. "It's not just about you, it's about my karma. That same good karma that'll help me get you a client at the last minute."

Her voice was firm and determined; Olivia had believed her. Perhaps it was a mistake, but what was another one? She'd just add it to the growing list, right there along with jeopardizing her reputation, embarrassing herself in front of a high-level journalist and kicking couture across the breakroom. Who knew couture could be so cutthroat.

She couldn't get much lower, that was for sure.

***

An hour later, Glory still hadn't called. Gladys had gone into comfort mode, trying to feed Olivia and Gwynnie. She watched as Olivia checked her phone . . . again.

"She'll call Mom."

"I don't know, Gwynnie."

"Eat your chicken," says Gladys, and Olivia takes a forkful from her barely touched plate.

Suddenly, Olivia's cell phone rings. The number on the caller I.D. doesn't come up. Olivia assumes it's an annoying sales call of some sort, or maybe some pollster calling to ask which way she was planning on voting in the next Presidential election. "Hello?" Silence from the other end. "Olivia? Is that you? The voice isn't completely recognizable. "It's Daphne, my darling! How are you? I received your very depressing voice message. Are you ok? I can tell something is wrong." Olivia was happy to hear from Daphne, but she was in one of those moods where she didn't feel like talking to anyone. "Hello Daphne! Oh, my goodness, how wonderful it is to hear from you! I am waiting for an important call and want to keep the line open. Could I call you back? How are you? I miss you!" After a few seconds of silence, Daphne answers, "But, of course darling. Absolutely anytime. My phone is always open, and I am always here for you. Though please know my number is now private so it won't show up when I call you. I just had to get rid of all of those spam calls. Why would I want to buy a timeshare in Ulan Bator? I mean maybe St. Barth's or Cartagena where it's chic and warm . . . though I do hear the nightlife is fabulous in Spain. What do you know about Portugal? Why is everyone buying real estate there? Come to think of it, a friend of a friend knows a real estate agent there . . . maybe I'll reach out. Oh God, I'm rambling . . . ok, I will text you my new cell number the second we hang up. I look forward to hearing everything. Please call as soon as you can! I know something is going on with you. I can sense it." Olivia, feeling terrible about cutting Daphne off tells her, "Thank you dear friend. I'm ok. I will call again soon. I love you!"

***

Olivia pushes the food around on her plate. Uninterested and nauseous with worry. "Don't be like that, Mom," says Gwynnie. "You'll get the call, and it'll be a great client."

"It's late, honey," says Olivia. "I think that ship has sailed."

"Don't give up Mom. Not yet. It'll work out."

"How do you know that?"

"Because you've worked so hard. You've earned it. And you're really, really good at this job."

Gladys nods. "You are. Still . . . I'd like to kill those girls. How dare they? So beneath you, Olivia. Now eat."

Olivia smiles.

After all they've been through, Gwynnie still has faith. She still believes good things happen to good people. And her mother is right there, rising to her defense.

"You don't believe me," says Gwynnie. "But that's okay. I'll believe for the both of us."

"What would I do without you honey?"

"I don't know," says Gwynnie, "But it would be a catastrophe, right?"

"Look," says Olivia, checking the time on her phone. "It's getting late, and there's no point in . . ."

As if on cue, the phone rings in her hand, a 917 area code popping up. Manhattan. She looks up at Gwynnie, eyes wide. *It couldn't be . . .*

"Told ya it would work out," says Gwynnie. "If you stop staring at me like that and answer it, I mean!"

"Hellllooooooo!" rings a voice. "Is this Olivia?"

"Yes, this is Olivia."

"Goooooood!" interrupts the caller. "Wonderful, that's just perfect! Olivia, I love that name! Oh, I haven't introduced myself, have I? Muffy Patton, Glory's friend. It's a delight, Olivia! and I just know we're destined to be friends. But where to start? There is so very, very much to discuss . . . ."

***

An hour later, Muffy finally gets to saying goodbye. "So, I'll see you tomorrow morning at 11:00. Can't wait! Toodles!"

Olivia hangs up and stares at her iPhone screen, shocked.

Gwynnie had been right, and Glory had risen to the occasion. An appointment had come through. Muffy was a real client, scheduled for tomorrow.

Olivia turns to Gwynnie and Gladys. "I guess . . . I have an appointment!"

Instantly, both are hugging her.

"Okay, okay," says Olivia, laughing. "I can't breathe! And I don't know if it'll mean anything, after what the reporter saw today."

"You'll make him forget all that," says Gladys confidently.

Olivia nods. "Well, I better go upstairs then. I've got to get some sleep."

Olivia couldn't believe it. Glory had come through. And based on her Google search, Muffy wasn't just a fill-in client, but a quality one. Her name came right up.

A well-maintained, well-established fifty-something, Muffy Patton's charitable endeavors, environmental activism, family money and Park Avenue Classic Six had all cemented herself amongst Manhattan's bohemia elite; several society page images even featured her looking buddy-buddy with Green Day's Billy Ray Armstrong.

True, she was a lot on the phone, talking a mile a minute, seemingly without a filter. *I'm just thrilled you can see me, Olivia!* she'd said, barely introducing herself before launching right in. *At first, I thought, what the hell? I was scheduled for Glory later this week, and now she wants to move me up and pass me off to someone else? You throwing me to the wolves, Glory? Who is this... Olivia? But she told me how remarkable you are, and about the journalist... and what can I say? I dig meeting new people and it is synchronicity, that's what I think. A fundraiser to launch my brand-new charitable foundation and a brand-new kindred spirit to make me look utterly fabulous! I believe in synchronicity, don't you?*

The woman was different, to say the least. By the time they were done, Olivia had said barely two dozen words, but heard Muffy's views on a variety of topics. Spiritual retreats (*just marvelous, getting in touch with your soul through fermenting leaves! And do avoid the nudist ones. A pinecone stuck to your bare ass can really hinder opening the chakras!*) to beauty maintenance (*Oxygen freezes? Given the state of our environment, we shouldn't waste our precious resources on beauty fads. Not that I'd ever reject an old-fashioned microdermabrasion.*)

to physical well-being (*Four words: organic high velocity colonic. Trust me on this.*)

In the hour-long one-sided conversation, at least Olivia had deduced the pertinent facts: the organization was called KarmaForKidz, and the fundraiser was black tie with a global twist. *Think a Sari, or one of those lovely Moroccan prints!* Muffy had said, throwing out ideas. *Native American-style, perhaps—I just adore fringe! Wait, is that appropriation? Shoot, I guess throw that last one out. And forget the next one right after I say it—a hajib, only in some marvelous, Versace-inspired fabric! I know, I know, we couldn't possibly. . . but wouldn't it be fabulous?*

Olivia had listened, amused, already pulling exotic, yet acceptable garments in her mind. She would make this woman feel gorgeous, fabulous . . . and she'd do it all with Blake watching.

Could it be? Olivia felt a sudden, unexpected spark of hope. A little flicker, no bigger than a single lighted match. *I have a client, at least. That was a big hurdle, but I jumped and cleared it. Who knows? Maybe this could work out. Maybe I could turn this into a high dollar, high UPT (units per transaction) sale.*

Glory had come through. Given up her own client for Olivia's sake. Olivia couldn't help but be touched, and the woman may be out there, one of Glory's classic space cadets, but . . . this might work. *A second chance to prove herself.*

Just as quickly, reality sets in. That tiny flickering match is extinguished by a virtual big ass bucket of ice water.

She has a new client tomorrow morning at 11 a.m.; the only time Muffy was available. 11 a.m.? That was mere hours away. Olivia didn't have time to strategize, let alone to pull clothes. She could come in to work early, but even then, she'll only have a small window. How will she prep in time? And then there are the other issues. The ones she cannot prepare for at all.

She's not prepared to step into that Salon again, head held high, like nothing happened. Never mind the overflowing bags of Amby's returns, *who knows what even happened with all of it after I left. . . no doubt Loss Prevention took it all back to the departments. Well, except for the stained pants . . . disgusting!* She'll be a one-woman army, storming enemy territory without any protection. In an instant, Olivia can picture how it will all go down, clear as an Alexis Bittar lucite cuff. She knows exactly what tomorrow will be like, down to what everyone will be thinking.

Gia. She might look at Olivia with a twinge of sympathy, but just that. Sure, *Chrissy was a bitch to set her up*, she might think. *But really . . . why would Olivia be foolish enough to trust her.* She needs to face the facts . . . this Salon job is not what she had anticipated. It's certainly not what she could have ever imagined it to be. So vicious.

Glory. Most likely, she will simply avoid Olivia. She'll scurry off quick as can be just like always. Only for once, she won't be wracked with guilt, just good karma, knowing she helped poor Olivia out. At the same time, she still won't take the risk of being associated with her.

Jasmin . . . who knows? Even when she's there, it isn't authentic, and she withdraws into her own isolated little world. When it comes to the Salon, sometimes she is even jealous, wishing she had a language barrier to fall back on.

Ursula. She'll just glance over, raise an eyebrow, stomp off to torture some new, young hopeful.

Then there are the most worrisome—Zoe and the C-Cups. Just the thought of facing them makes Olivia's skin crawl. Who knows what they will do? Maybe roll their eyes, or stare at her blankly. Giggle, whisper or just blatantly ignore her. That'll be the icing on her humiliation, for sure. Or maybe they'll find a new way to sabotage her . . . she wouldn't put it past them.

Olivia throws herself across her bed, arm across her eyes.

She can't pull this off. There isn't time, she isn't ready. What Olivia needs is help, advice. She needs a revelation, that's it. Some divine intervention . . .

"Ollllivvvia!"

Olivia sits upright. "Mom?" *Thanks a lot, universe. That's all you got?*

"Where are you . . . oh! There you are."

"You knew I was here."

"Finish your prep?"

Olivia groans. "This isn't a colonoscopy, though it sure feels like it could be."

"Oh, Olivia, I can tell just by looking at your face. You're having second thoughts. Worries. A mother knows these things, Olivia."

"It's just too much. They hate me. This is a losing battle, Mom. I don't know what to do."

"Yes, you do," says Gladys, her voice surprisingly calm. She sits on the bed. "You only have one option."

"What's that?"

"You just have to go in there and wow the hell out of everyone. Be so extraordinary with this new client that they completely forget what happened today. Don't tell me what you can't do. Show these bloodsucking tics what you *can* do!"

Olivia almost laughs. "Is that all?"

"You've been through enough, Olivia, I have faith. You can pull this off."

Olivia is completely taken aback.

"I believe in your capabilities. Don't look so shocked." Gladys stares at the wall, sadness in her eyes. "I know I'm not always the easiest mother, Olivia. I demanded a great deal of you. Too much, not that it helps you now. I realized it far too late." She shakes her head. "I often wonder if that's why you ended up with . . . you know."

He'd been dead more than six months, and she still couldn't say his name.

"Perhaps that's why you chose someone like him. Someone who expected perfection. Because I put that expectation on you." She looks at Olivia, eyes wet. "It was my fault, perhaps. That everything ended up this way."

"Oh my God, Mom. You can't be serious. You didn't make me fall in love with him. I mean, c'mon . . . you're talking next level Jewish guilt."

"I pushed you away!"

"You didn't push me away, I just got swept away by . . . a sociopath. I was young, and he was rich and romantic and . . . before I knew it, I was becoming this completely other person. It had nothing to do with . . .

look, my choices were my choices. I'm the one who picked my own path, Mom. I picked Edwin."

She winces at his name, and Olivia can see she is holding back tears.

"Mom, I promise you," Olivia says, reaching out to touch her hand. "It wasn't your fault. "I know you think the world revolves around you, but guess what? You aren't that important."

"Oh, thanks a lot," says Gladys, though she gives a small smile.

"And yeah, you are tough and demanding . . . you have always expected a lot of me. But you also taught me to be strong, just like you. That's the reason I've kept going, even after losing everything. Because you taught me to be like that. Not to quit, no matter how hard things get."

"Which is exactly what you'll do tomorrow."

"I wish it were that easy."

"Please. You can win over that journalist again. I have no doubt. If you can win over those DC society social climbers, this guy will be no problem. Besides, you can charm anyone. You get that innate skill from me."

Olivia laughs. "Well, he did seem to respect me. Right before Zoe and her coven of den bitches."

"Oh, and I have a few words about them," cuts in Gladys. Olivia cannot help but smile. "As for those bratty, conspiring little predators, you know their problem? Terrible mothers. What were their names? Chloe, Catie and Cassy?"

"Close enough."

"Mmmm-hmmm. Waspy snobs, I suspect, probably raised by nannies. With girls like that, there's only one way to get the upper hand: you ignore their very existence."

"It isn't that easy, you know, Mom."

"Of course, it is! Besides, who are they, anyway? Not fit to lick your Louboutin's. The ones you scuffed. Don't think I didn't notice."

"Sorry about that."

Gladys waves her off. "And here's what it comes down to, darling. For all their sabotaging-yimmer-yammer yenta-ing, you have something those girls will never have. It's the very reason they despise you."

Olivia snorts. "What could I possibly have that they don't?"

"Olivia! Talent. You have talent! All kinds of it! The Salon is lucky to have you, don't forget that. Just go in and remind them who they are dealing with. You are a Kopelman, Olivia. You have style in your bones." Gladys stands up, straightens her skirt and raises an eyebrow. "So what? You plan on sitting there moping for the rest of the night? Get to it! You have work to do."

Chapter Three

At 10:10 a.m. Olivia heads down 5th Avenue with a fresh attitude, lipstick applied in YSL's Rose Celebration (purchased with the employee 20% discount) in an entirely new outfit and plenty of time to spare. Okay, so the outfit isn't new in the classic sense, it is vintage, but it's new to Olivia and she knows it looks good. Chanel, of course, and hand-picked by Gladys.

"One of my favorites," Gladys had said, appearing with a garment bag that morning.

"You're full of surprises. I've never seen it?"

"No, not this one. Perhaps the most valuable in my collection—I planned on giving it to you for a very special occasion."

"Which one?"

"My funeral, if you really want to know. I assume you'll be overwhelmed, but I can't have my daughter looking frumpy on such a momentous day. But tomorrow will be tremendously momentous as well, so what the hell? You can wear it for both."

Olivia shook her head. "You're crazy, Mom."

"I suppose. But when it comes to fashion, I have an eye. Just like you."

Now, heading towards Harper James, Olivia feels entirely transformed. On the surface, the suit is simple. A black knee-length, slim A-line skirt and matching iconic jacket, the tiny gold buttons engraved with the interlocking C's. Yet, Olivia knows the divine attention paid to every detail, from the silk lining to every precise stitch. To some, the jacket is simply tweed, but Olivia knows differently—to make the unique pattern, it takes up to twelve varieties of thread and 16 total panels; eight in the front and eight in the back; the same with the interior lining. Each jacket has four pockets- iconic to Coco's desire for intricate spaces to keep her lipstick, her cigarettes. It is magical—originally inspired by menswear, specifically that of the Duke of Westminster. Each jacket adorns a delicate chain sewn through the interior along the bottom edge, making certain the jacket fits and falls perfectly against the body. This same chain echoes that of the 2.55, Olivia's best and last investment to her superficial self. The jacket, like the bag, isn't showy or over-the-top; there are no overt embellishments or hints of ostentatious bling.

It looks perfect with Gladys's Chanel two-toned camel and black heels. Fortunately, Olivia and Gladys wear the same size. 39.5.

Just knowing the craftsmanship she is wearing, Olivia stands taller, walks with a confident stride. Even the day is playing along, the icy wind replaced with a crisp breeze, a hint of sun peeping out, like a real-life PR promo for a pre-Spring runway collection.

Olivia was up late preparing, but she feels wide awake. Every piece is in place, every moment perfectly timed. Now all she needs to do is let go of her anxiety, keep her mind on the task ahead and remain completely and utterly calm.

Yeah, right. And she's the former Queen of England, herself.

Just make it through today without being sabotaged, losing my shit or embarrassing myself in front of Blake, she thinks. She checks her phone again. 10:20 a.m. Ten minutes to D-Day.

Olivia pushes down her nerves, reminding herself she is ready. Everything has been planned, her schedule perfectly timed. She quickly runs through the details one last time in her head, just like the night of that dreaded and deadly dinner party:

10:30—meet Blake outside the main doors.

That had been easy—she'd texted him early that morning. *Turns out my appointment is at 11:00*, she'd written, *I need to pull a few extra garments beforehand. Thought you might like to come along for a backstage tour?*

He'd written back immediately. *Sounds great!*

10:45—pick up rack.

She hadn't pulled any garments at all; she'd pulled a favor instead. The email, sent at 3:00 a.m., was titled *Last Minute Favor (I'll Owe You Big Time).*

Ruby, I would never ask this of you last minute, but it's an emergency . . . I'll explain later. But I need to get these items pulled for a last-minute surprise client by 10:45 a.m.! I'm freaking out, but, if you can help me, I swear I'll be eternally grateful and buy you the biggest steak and champagne dinner on Earth . . . The Palm, Fogo de Chao, M&S—your pick.

She'd spent several hours compiling the specifics, relying on her memory and the Harper James website for reference. In the end, she'd come up with a good list, the pieces embracing Muffy's free-spirited quirkiness, yet adding a sophisticated edge. The choices were exotic, just as Muffy requested, only tasteful homage instead of potential offense. Roberto Cavalli in bold flower prints, an African-inspired Diane Von Furstenberg, a Ralph Lauren batik maxi dress, enough animal print pieces to make up for DC's National Zoo.

By the time she finished and pressed send, she was exhausted. She'd crashed for a few hours, then woken up and checked her email first thing. There was one from Ruby right at the top, short and sweet:

Olivia, no prob! Anything for you! Ruby

10:55—arrive at Salon lobby

She and Blake would greet Muffy in the Salon lobby, rack in hand. She'd officially introduce the journalist. Muffy had seemed excited at the concept during their phone conversation. *The more the merrier!* she'd told Olivia. *Tell me, is he handsome? Men of letters are the sexiest thing, right?* Olivia had no idea what she might say to Blake in person, but chances are it would be unconventional.

This was a good thing, Olivia had decided. *Colorful characters could only make his article better.*

11:00—Enter Salon.

Olivia would stride inside, a bright smile on her face, with the client, journalist and rack of ready-to-wear in tow. She'd be chatting pleasantly, like she didn't have a care in the world. Of course, there would be shocked expressions, whispers and glares, but she wouldn't acknowledge them, simply turning away. No need for public declarations or explanations of any kind; her presence would say it all. *See? You don't have the power to destroy me. Try to push me down, and I'll only get up stronger and look fabulous in Chanel.*

The schedule served two purposes—avoid being alone in the Salon and make an entrance that counted.

Reaching Harper James, she checks her phone—10:30 on the dot. And Blake is on time too. Thank the fashion gods. Waiting at the crosswalk, she sees him across the street. Wearing a navy sweater and the same jeans, he is drinking coffee next to a cart and chatting with someone she knows—Willard. He says something, and it must be funny, because Willard laughs. Blake grins, and he looks so friendly and approachable that for a second Olivia forgets the power he holds. To make or break her, and the Salon. To portray both in any way he desires.

To share that portrayal with a mass audience. But she has this power, too, she reminds herself. She is no fish-handshake-wallflower.

She crosses the street and Blake spots her right away. "Hi!' he says, grinning. "Ready to do this again?"

"You bet she is," says Willard, giving her a covert wink. "Our Olivia can handle anything."

Maybe it is seeing Willard, a friendly face, and getting that last-minute boost. Or maybe it is the validation of those she loves. Her mother's knowing smile as she dictated her belief about Olivia as though undisputed fact.

You are a Kopelman, Olivia. You have style in your bones.

Maybe it's Olivia's hopefulness, or her extensive preparations. Or maybe . . . it's simply the Chanel.

Whatever the reason, the day has just begun, and Olivia is nailing it. And she's doing it effortlessly, by just being herself. As she and Blake head to the 5th floor, their conversation is free-flowing and easy—no mention of the way yesterday ended. Instead, he's easy to talk to . . . funny, curious . . . though not in an obtrusive way. In the elevator, she gives a quick rundown of her newest client.

"She's a bit eccentric," Olivia explains. "No filter, I suppose you might say, but in a charming way. And a huge heart; her charity work is very important to her."

"So, how do you do it, then? How do you choose the clothes?"

"For her, or in general?"

"Both."

"That's an intricate question," says Olivia, as they exit the elevator, and Olivia leads him through the maze of aisles. "I guess I take stock of the client's needs first. She has lots of events, for example. Black tie kinds of things. Then I think about the image they need to portray and their personal style. Muffy's tastes tend towards the dramatic . . . she likes an international flavor, an exotic flair. Of course, it can't be so extreme that people will be afraid to write checks, but her quirkiness is engaging. She's fun . . . a free spirit . . . I'd never try to stifle that. Being a good personal shopper isn't about turning a client into someone else but taking the best parts of someone and actualizing them in a physical way. Wow, did that make any sense?"

"Completely. In fact, I've never heard it put that way. It's pretty deep, actually."

"Skin deep, maybe," says Olivia, laughing. "It's not philosophy, I know that. Change the whole way you see yourself and the world. It can be transformative." Olivia stops suddenly, seeing a familiar location. "Wow, speaking of transformative," she says, almost to herself. Without making a conscious decision, she has taken the long route, which leads them through the most isolated back corner of the women's department. A good choice, this isolation, considering the noise.

They have suddenly been surrounded by a wall of blaring pop music. Olivia knows this place, but a different version. She stands there, stunned.

The La'Airy department, only completely recreated.

Olivia hasn't been here in a while, and the last time it had still been in transition. Totally cleared, just an empty sales desk, bare racks and a *Pardon The Dust, Exciting Things Coming Soon!* sign.

Seems they've come, and exciting is one word to describe it.

Along with the new soundtrack, other changes—gone are the tasteful pieces in classic silhouettes, the well-made simplicity harkening back to an earlier time. The neutrals and soft pastels have been replaced with fiery reds, hot pinks and dayglo yellow; timeless cocktail dresses, cashmere sweaters and subtle silver accessories traded for low-cut and cut-outs, lace accents and laced-up bustiers. It is a garish carnival of sequins, fringe and mesh bodycon. It hurts Olivia's eyes.

A few girls mill about, none looking older than a tween, gossiping and giggling over possibilities. "OMG, this is so extra!" squeals one, holding up a backless halter dress with a plunging neckline.

"That is lit," says her friend, snapping her gum. "You're gonna look like sex on a stick!"

Judging by the braces and carefully concealed acne, they can't be older than thirteen.

"Riviera Detroit," says Olivia, reading the lettering on the wall. "I've never heard of them."

"Her," says Blake. "She's a tween television star. She's also got a hit single and line of appetite suppressant lollipops." Olivia looks at him, eyebrows raised. He shrugs. "My editor wanted me to cover her new fashion label for a trends piece, but I politely declined."

"Smart move," says Olivia.

"What was this place before?"

"La'Airy. The department I started in."

"I always liked La'Airy. Too bad they've taken a downward turn. My mother and grandmother both wore La'Airy. Well-made pieces. Timeless, right?"

"Absolutely," says Olivia. "But I guess their time was up."

Marcus Courtney, thinks Olivia. *This is his work.*

In front of her, the girl has discarded her first dress, replacing it with a pleated one so mini, it practically doesn't exist. "This is what they replaced La'Airy with?" she says, suddenly angry. "What Marguerite was right sized for?"

"Marguerite?"

Shit. Olivia hadn't even realized she said the words out loud.

"Sorry, it's nothing," says Olivia, checking her phone. 10:45 a.m. "C'mon, we better go. We've got an appointment to make."

***

Ruby is ready for them. "Just give me a sec," she says, rushing to the back. She returns with Olivia's selections carefully lined up on a rolling rack.

"Thank you so much, Ruby!"

"Anything for you," says the girl, grinning. She turns to Blake. "You're the journalist, right?"

"Wow, word travels fast. Yes, I'm a journalist."

"Well, you're lucky to follow Olivia. We all love her down here."

Olivia is stunned, unsure whether to be flattered or embarrassed. "I paid her to say that" she quips. "Well, we better get moving!"

"You guys know each other long?" asks Blake.

Uh-oh, thinks Olivia, pushing the rolling rack towards the aisle and hoping Blake will get the hint.

"Not too long. It's funny, since I met her after she moved upstairs." Fuck, thinks Olivia, hoping that one just slid by.

"Why is that funny? Don't you talk to the other women who work at the Salon?" Blake asks.

She should have known better. Ruby bites her lip, suddenly concerned she messed up. She looks from Blake to Olivia. Too late now, Olivia thinks, giving Ruby a resigned shrug.

"Talk to them? Ha. As if they'd lower themselves like that. But Olivia, she's different. She's not a snob. She's great, right?" Ruby grins. "All I'm saying, Mr. Journalist, is we love her down here and your article better make her look good."

Blake smiles. "Mind if I quote you on that, Miss . . .?"

"Hernandez. And sure thing."

"Let me just write that down," says Blake, grabbing a mini-sized notebook from his pocket and quickly jotting down some notes. *Sorry*, mouths Ruby over his head and Olivia smiles and waves it off. Then she looks down at Blake and back at Olivia, raises her eyebrows and mouths three words.

He's totally hot.

***

When they are safely on the service elevator, rolling rack in tow, Olivia nonchalantly checks her cell. 10:55 a.m. Despite the distraction, they are still on schedule.

"I finally learned your secret," says Blake.

"Oh? What could that be?" she says nonchalantly, though her pulse has gone into full-throttle acceleration mode. *Which secret? The con ex-husband, the lost fortune, the new identity? Well, old identity, really. But still, it's a lie. Or maybe it's her qualification for this job, how truly lacking they are . . .*

"People *like* you. A lot. Between Willard and Ruby, you've got a full-fledged Olivia Kopelman fan club."

Thank God.

"I don't know about all that. They're just good people."

"Are you friendly with the girls in the Salon as well?"

Olivia paused, though just for a second. "I keep it professional."

Olivia stares at the elevator buttons, watching them light up as they rise. Without turning, she knows he is watching her. "You're mysterious, Olivia."

"Me? No way."

"So . . . where are you from originally?"

"New Jersey. No mystery there." She turns to him with a smile. "Good thing, since the article is about the Salon and not me," she says, keeping her voice light and teasing.

"Sure," he says, grinning back, and Olivia realizes something with a start. Ruby was right. He is kind of hot. Not in a slick, obvious way, like Marcus, but the kind that creeps up on you, hidden beneath his easy manner, his effortless charm. A slow burn kind of hot as haphazard as his disheveled hair and 501 jeans. The same ones he wore yesterday, Olivia is pretty sure. She wonders if he is going commando.

"I was just curious," he says. "Not journalist curious, the personal kind."

A ding and the elevator stops. As the doors whoosh open, Olivia shouts, "Here we are!" and defiantly pushes the rack ahead. "Don't want to be late for Muffy!"

Guys like him are hot, sure. But let down your defenses, reveal too much, and you might get burned. *Publicly.*

Focus on what matters, thinks Olivia, as she and Blake head down the long hallway towards the Salon. She knows she should be nervous, facing those vindictive bitches again, but for some reason, she feels totally calm. She remembers her lipstick and quickly and quietly applies another layer of a Duane Reade discounted find, Rose Celebration.

At the Salon door, she tries to navigate the doorknob and rack. "Hey, let me get that," says Blake, stepping ahead. Olivia smiles at him, thinking, *I'm going to nail this. I'm going to meet Muffy and she's going to love . . .*

Only there's no one inside. "She must be running late," says Olivia, telling herself not to panic. *No big deal, clients are late all the time.*

Okay, so it won't be the big entrance she imagined, but it will work. Just act nonchalantly, not a care in the world. *Come in chatting! That's even better!* "I'm sure she'll be here soon," she says, opening the Salon door.

"You thirsty? We have everything you could imagine in the breakroom."

The second she is inside, before even turning from Blake, she knows something is off. Perhaps it is the noise, or lack thereof. Heart beating fast, Olivia turns slowly around.

They are all staring at her, just as expected. Gia, Ursula, Jasmin. Only none have the expressions she predicted. Instead of judgmental glares, they look confused. Concerned, even.

What's going on?

Squeals of excitement rise, breaking the silence. Everyone turns in unison towards the source—it is coming from Zoe's area. She and the C's are gathered around the platform, where an older client is modeling a voluminous blue dress. Even from behind, Olivia can tell it is shapeless—not even ill-fitting but lacking any fit at all. The kind of shapeless, layered shift you'd pick for a heavy-set older woman if you have no idea what an older heavy-set woman might look good in. A passive and ill-thought-out selection.

"Adorable!" says Chrissy.

"Really gorge!" agrees Catie, both with overly enthusiastic, plastered on party smiles. They turn to Zoe, awaiting the final verdict.

"Lovely," she says. "Very fetching."

"Totally!" echo the C-Cups.

"I just don't know, girls." Olivia knows that voice. "Isn't it a little, I don't know, post-menopausal-Idaho-potato-sack?"

"Not at all," sings Zoe. "It's elegant. And wait till you see it with the accessories!"

The woman turns to the three upturned, young, admiring faces. "Well, why not? Let's give it a try."

It can't be her; she thinks. Though she already knows the answer, just as she knew the voice. It is the same voice she listened to for an hour on the phone. And that face is the one she saw smiling from society shots. Once, even, with Beyonce.

A chill runs through Olivia, from unpainted toenails to non-waxed eyebrows.

"Olivia," hisses a voice, making her turn with a start. To her left is Glory, eyes wide with apologetic horror."

"I was just about to call you . . . oh my God, Olivia. I just got here too . . . I didn't have time to stop it!" says Glory frantically, her voice growing louder. "You have to understand."

She should have expected this.

"I would never, ever have let this happen if I'd been around! But by the time I got here, it was too late."

Fucking Zoe! Olivia feels the rage rise, threatening to blow. She wants to march over and rip apart that conniving backstabber!

No. Keep it together, Olivia. Don't give her what she wants. Don't make this worse.

Olivia glances over her shoulder—across the room, Blake stands by himself, flipping through pages, reviewing his previous notes. He looks calm and unobtrusive, seemingly unaware of the drama unfolding in front of them. But by now, Olivia knows how sharp he is—Blake isn't missing a second, not a word.

There's no time for anger or retribution—*later*, she tells herself. Right now, keep it together. *Most of all, keep this from becoming an embarrassing scene.*

"It's okay, Glory," she says calmly. "I'm sure it wasn't your fault."

"I swear, Olivia," says Glory, tears rising. "When I got here, she was already with them. You hadn't gotten here, and I suspect Zoe jumped on her the second she arrived."

"Oh, Olivia! You're here!"

So much for crisis management. Zoe is floating in her direction, angelically smiling and stopping a foot away from Olivia, "There you are!"

Olivia knows all the eyes that are focused on her, all the breaths that are being held in . . . everyone watching and waiting for the inevitable—her explosion.

"Yes," says Olivia matter-of-factly. "Here I am."

"Oh my gosh, I'm so glad! There has been a slight change of itinerary. I met Muffy earlier today, and . . ." she turns. "Muffy, Olivia is here!"

At the platform, Muffy looks up from the several scarves Chrissy is showing her. "Olivia!" she says, stepping down. She heads over, already talking a mile a minute. "Oh, how lovely to meet you in person! Though I feel like I know you already," she says, going in for air kisses.

"Nice to meet you too, Muffy!"

"And now, I can put a voice to the face! And what a lovely face. Everyone here is just so lovely, so vivacious! You all make me feel elderly, just ancient! How do you stand it, Glory?"

"I avoid them," deadpans Glory, to which Muffy gives a barking laugh.

"Yup, we sure are the old broads! But it's lovely, all this youth. What a lark! And . . . oh, Olivia!" she says, suddenly realizing something. "I hope you don't mind! I know we had an appointment, but I met Zoe in the waiting room. She seemed so nice. So welcoming."

You mean she accosted you?

"And, of course, I know her mother from the charity circuit. I mean, we've never actually been formally introduced before."

"You two will love each other," pipes in Zoe. "I cannot wait to introduce you." Zoe gives her a glowing smile, which Muffy seems to bask in. "She's very generous, your mother. Just like you!"

Generous enough to write a check, I bet. Made out to KarmaForKidz.

"Well, we just clicked! And she had some wonderful ideas for the gala."

Like that blue potato sack you're wearing.

"You don't mind, do you?"

Before Olivia can even open her mouth, Zoe gives a high-pitched squeal, her tiny French manicured hand clapping to her mouth. "Oh no!" she says, eyes wide. "I completely forgot! The reporter! Oh no, Olivia. Is he here?"

It's so over-the-top, the performance, Olivia almost laughs. She wouldn't get cast as an understudy extra in a Lifetime movie, it's that bad. Zoe scans the room in faux panic. "Oh shoot!" she says, spotting Blake in exactly the spot where she knew he was. "Oh no. He was supposed to follow you, right?"

Olivia is exhausted. By all of it.

"He can just follow you," she says. Her voice, calm and matter of fact. Then, quietly, "That was your intention, wasn't it, Zoe?"

For a moment, Zoe looks confused. She got what she wanted, but too easily. Then, like in slow motion, it sinks in: Olivia has had the audacity to call her out.

"That's a great idea, Olivia," she says, loud enough for everyone to hear. She turns to Blake, all smiles. "Blake . . . that's your name, right?"

He looks up from his notes, eyebrows raised. "Sure is. And you're Zoe, right?"

She smiles, pleased. "Yes, we were never formally introduced."

He puts away the notebook and walks over, taking his time. He raises a hand. "Nice to meet you," he says. "Formally."

"You too," she purrs, gazing up from under her phony eyelashes. There are so many versions of Zoe, but this one she recognizes immediately. Olivia's seen it once before, when Marcus was around. "It seems we have a little issue, though. You were going to observe Olivia's fitting today, right?"

"I was."

"Well, unfortunately, there was a slight mix-up." She goes on to explain, doing her best, *oh-gosh-shucks-my-silly-mistake,* Olivia has to admit she's good. The lilting voice, the big eyes—she can't *believe* this happened, she's *so* embarrassed, she and Muffy just got along so well and next thing you know . . .

It's all an act, Olivia knows that, but she has it down to a tee. In that moment, Olivia sees it clearly. It is an act so perfectly constructed, so refined, so manipulative . . . well, Olivia could never have won, not really. Not with all the preparation and talent in the world.

Zoe is the human version of an Instagram post that has been carefully staged, a configuration of *The Rules*, Cosmo Tips and reality dating show editing all in one. From the worried lip bite to the meaningful eye contact, she's got the act down. Cute, with a side of sex appeal; helpless, yet in complete control. The girl may be a ruthless tyrant with sociopathic tendencies, but she's convincing. So much so, Olivia almost believes the story herself.

"So, Olivia just had a great idea," she finishes. "Just follow me! Maybe it will give you another perspective for your article."

Olivia never stood a chance. Admitting it is almost a relief.

Blake turns to her. "What about all the clothes you pulled?"

Olivia shrugs and smiles. "It's okay," she says.

"I don't know. I had planned on following several fittings with the same shopper."

Olivia can feel Zoe's agitation growing. He should have given into her right away . . . that's what she's thinking.

"The article is about the Salon, right?" says Olivia, just wanting this to end. "Zoe's been here longer than I have, so you'll get to see it from another point of view."

"Exactly," says Zoe, now annoyed. "Besides, you need to observe clients, right? Well, I have one, and Olivia doesn't. So . . ."

"She can have mine."

Olivia looks up, confused. Who said that?

"A writer should stick to their vision. She can have my client." All faces turn to one direction . . . Jasmin. "I don't mind, really. And neither will she." Jasmin glances at her watch. "She'll be here at two."

Chapter Four

Ten minutes later, outside Harper James, Olivia and Jasmin stand on the Fifth Avenue sidewalk, staring at each other in silence. Around them, lunch hour is in full swing—nannies pushing UPPA Baby strollers, tourists tote FAO Schwartz shopping bags and guys in three-piece Canali super 300 suits joking around as they head to their lunch meetings at Le Bernardin and Aquavit. "Excuse me," says a woman, dodging them as she speed-walks by in a business skirt suit and Nike white sneakers.

Finally, Jasmin grins. "Did you see Zoe's face? I swear, that whore practically shit herself." Suddenly, both are laughing. They laugh so hard a passing man mutters, *Freaks*.

"I'm starving," says Jasmin when they finally get control. "I'm dying for a hot dog."

***

It happened so fast—first, Jasmin making her pronouncement, then Blake thanking her. "That really would be better," he said. Then Jasmin telling Olivia they should do a quick client run-down, so she'd be prepared, and Blake saying no problem, he could go grab lunch and be back in plenty of time for Olivia's two o'clock.

Olivia had watched the whole thing, utterly shocked. *She had a client.* And more importantly, *Jasmin spoke English?* Perfect English, in fact.

Equally as shocked was Zoe. At first, she'd tried to intervene, saying there was no need, Muffy was right here and ready to go.

"I think it's better if I stick with Olivia," Blake had said. His voice firm, sealing the deal.

All settled, he excused himself, heading for the Salon door.

The instant he was gone, reality set in, Olivia watching as Zoe's confusion turned to horror, then hate. The last one aimed in one direction—Olivia.

"You set me up," she hissed.

Before Olivia could say she was wrong—if anyone had been set up, it was Olivia herself—Zoe had already spun on her heels, storming towards the breakroom, concerned C's in tow.

With Ursula and Gia off in a corner, deep into their smart phones, space had cleared. Only two remained—Jasmin and Olivia, contemplating each other across the polished wood floor.

"C'mon," Jasmin had said. "I really need to get the hell out of here."

***

Only after Jasmin has bought a hot dog with the works, and they've found an empty bench outside a busy midtown dry cleaning operation, does Olivia finally say what she has been thinking.

"Please don't take this the wrong way, but . . . I didn't think you spoke much English."

"Good," says Jasmin, wiping mustard from her mouth. "That was my intention."

"Wait . . . do the other girls know?"

"Beats me. Now they do, for sure. I started six months ago, and by then Zoe and her little sidekick party girl kiss-asses had already been around a while. Not terribly long, but long enough to have taken over the place. She never saw me as a threat, I guess, since Middle Eastern clients are my specialty . . . I mean, that's where I grew up. But, putting me in a box like that, well . . . it really pissed me off."

"What country did you grow up in?"

"All over. I was born in Egypt, but we lived in Saudi Arabia for a while. Dubai when I was a teenager. That's where I first discovered fashion. I'm also good at languages, so I picked up quite a few. French, English, Italian, German, Turkish. Arabic, of course."

"Wow, you moved a lot."

"My father was a commercial architect. Very successful. Every time he got a new major commission, we'd relocate, but he refused to send me off to boarding school like all the other rich kids I knew. He just put me in different local private schools. Hey, sure you're not hungry? This thing is delish . . . especially with this extra spicy German mustard . . . OMG, are we in Munich? Achtung! I could really go for a beer right about now."

"No way," says Olivia. "My stomach is full of butterflies—I could go for a glass of anything right now. Guess I'm still in shock. But, please, tell me more."

As she lavishes over and finally finishes her heavily delicious hot dog, Jasmin goes on to explain that when she first moved to New York, her clients were the women she'd known growing up—now adults, they not only had family money, but many had married into even more wealth. "They come to New York often, sometimes just to shop. So, when I moved here and started styling, it was a natural client base. I was at Saks for a while, then Bloomingdales . . . and when Harper James recruited me, I thought, why not? I'd heard they were having trouble, and I knew it was less about my talent and more about my built-in client base, but . . . honestly,

I didn't give a flip. I mean, Harper James is iconic, right? A bastion of refinement and good taste." She dabs her mouth, crinkles the wrapper, lifts her arm and aims. "Then I met Zoe." She aims and purposefully throws the balled-up trash, as they both watch it arc through the air and land right into the trash can. "What a bitch."

"I couldn't agree more."

"Yup, you know better than anyone." Jasmin leans back and contemplates her for a second. "First week, no one said a word to me."

"Sounds familiar."

"But I was busy with clients right away, so it didn't matter. It did give me a chance to observe the place, see how it works. Kind of like your first week, right?" She gives Olivia a knowing look. "I knew exactly how you felt, sitting behind that desk, watching how everything went down. I felt badly for you, because I'd been there. Only in my case, after watching me deal with clients for a week, talking to them in French, Arabic . . . well, Zoe finally decided I wasn't a threat and came up to introduce herself, passive aggressive as hell. Talking about how great it was, that there was someone willing to deal with my type of clients, blah blah, how exhausting it must be, yadda yadda, how high maintenance they are . . . you get it. Just standard stereotypical BS. She's so full of it herself, that A#1 bi-otch."

Olivia shakes her head, imagining the scene. Zoe saying all those things in her sweet voice, with a condescending smile. "So, I listened to the whole thing, not saying a word. Just stared at her. Finally, when she was uber uncomfortable, she had a revelation. *Oh! You don't speak much English, do you?* I thought, *no, I just don't speak English, you horrible person.* By the end of the day, she'd spread the word, and I figured, this is the best thing that could happen. By then, I knew that place was toxic, but it was too late to back out. So, the only English I've spoken since then is the broken kind, and only when forced. Until today."

"But . . . after this, Zoe will torture you."

"I put in my thirty day notice two weeks ago, Olivia. I'm on my way out. So big deal, I speed it up by a week. Totally worth it. Solely for the look on her face!" Jasmin laughs, relishing the moment.

"You're leaving?"

"I'm getting married, moving back to Dubai."

"Oh my God, congratulations! Mazel Tov!"

"Thank you. Funny, I came halfway around the world to fall in love with a guy I knew in high school. But he's amazing, and I can keep my styling business overseas. I don't have to—between you and me, he's filthy rich. A businessman, Dubai is his home base. But I told him, I'm not giving up my career. You marry me, that's part of the deal. He said okay right away . . . he's head over heels." She giggles. "Honestly, so am I."

"I'm so happy for you!"

"Thanks. And I don't mind moving. I've always loved Dubai."

"But I still don't understand . . . why did you do this for me? I mean, we hardly know each other."

"I know you better than you think. I know they hate you because you're good at this job. I've watched them torture you and, today with the reporter, that was as low as it gets. That was your opportunity, not hers. She deserved to lose it and get called out."

"That's so nice, but . . . you did all that? For me?"

"Actually, no. That was just the icing on top. The real reason? To see her expression. Finally, she knows what it feels like."

"What's that?"

"Humiliation." Jasmin grins. "And you know what? It was the highlight of my Harper James tenure, hands down."

By the time they say goodbye, it's already 1:30. "So, the rack of clothes is by my desk, and you'll like the Princess, trust me."

"I can't believe this . . . she's a real princess? And she really doesn't mind a replacement personal shopper?" says Olivia. She'd watched as Jasmin called the princess to explain why Olivia needed to take over her appointment—even though she hadn't understood what they were saying, it seemed to have gone well—at least, Jasmin had laughed quite a bit during the short conversation.

"She thinks it's hilarious, actually. She comes to New York to shop every few months, so it isn't that big of a deal. We've been friends since we were kids, and we talk all the time, so she is well aware of the Harper James situation. We spend half the appointments making fun of Zoe and her lapdogs in Arabic. She'll tell me what Zoe is doing at that moment, like a running commentary. *Now the dumb white girl is putting on pink lip gloss, now the dumb white girl is calling her boyfriend to offer blowjob services* . . . it's hard to translate, but she thinks the girl is trash. And she calls Chrissy and Catie the double-tittied monster."

"That's even better than the C-Cups!" says Olivia, laughing. "That's what I call them in my head."

Jasmin laughs. "God, the best part of leaving . . . never having to see those girls again."

"So, the princess . . . is there anything I should know? Should I call her Your Royal Highness?"

"We are familiar, but as an outsider, you need to show respect for her status. Tell her how honored you are to dress her. That kind of thing. She'll warm up to you quickly, I'm sure. And Olivia?"

"Yes?"

"If she comes off a little uptight at first, don't be surprised. She might make a big entrance, but that's just her way. She always has security with her, too . . . just ignore them. I do. She'll warm up to you, I promise." Jasmin smiles. "Just like I did."

"Jasmin, I don't know."

"From that very first day, I liked you. Don't thank me, Olivia, take this as an apology. For leaving you out there on your own with those wild and reckless animals." She pauses, thinking. "We're too good for that place, you know. I just hope you realize it way sooner than I did."

***

Fifteen minutes before the appointment, Blake meets Olivia outside Harper James. "Deja vu," he says, pushing open the door for her. They head towards the elevator, Olivia silently waiting for the questions to come. *What was that scene upstairs? Are clients often passed around like chewing gum? Are all personal shopping departments dens of abject chaos, extreme dysfunction and hyper-elevated hormonal emotion?*

"You know what I don't understand?" he says, once they are inside the elevator and rising. "Why don't men wear suspenders anymore?"

Olivia looks at him, eyebrows raised.

"Not that I'd wear them myself or anything," he continues. "A jacket is as far as I'll go, and only when required. But suspenders, they're cool. So why?"

"Many do. Perhaps not daily, but special occasions for sure."

"I see. Guess it's hard to tell since they aren't meant to be seen."

Olivia laughs. "You work at a fashion journal, right?"

"Fell into it, what can I say? Just a freelance gig, but they liked my approach. Then it became full time. Since I didn't have the background, I had to learn quickly. So anytime I have a question, I ask."

"I noticed that."

"Funny thing, though . . . people don't do that in this industry, do they? They'd rather stumble in the dark than admit they don't know it all." He grins at her. "It isn't just about putting on clothes, I think. It's putting on a whole persona."

The elevator stops.

"That's why you're the perfect person to follow," he says, stepping out. "You are totally yourself. Authentic."

If only you knew.

"That's a compliment, right?"

"It would be if I liked you . . . which I do."

Much to her chagrin, Olivia feels herself blush. *What am I doing?* She thinks, then chastises herself. He's just trying to warm her up, charm his way into a good story.

Luckily, the hallway to the salon is too dim to notice. Thank God for mood lighting.

"Isn't that against the rules? Liking the subject of the story," she says, picking up her pace towards the Salon. Hurriedly, she applies another layer of today's armor, berry blush.

"You aren't the subject, right? Or so you continually remind me," he says, and she feels him watching her, a smile on his face. "This is about the Salon."

"Speaking of . . . here we are."

Outside the lobby door, she feels a burst of nervous energy, then reminds herself everything will be fine. *There can only be so many dramas in one day*, she thinks and hopes, while opening the door and motioning to Blake. "After you."

"So," he says, stepping inside, "Tell me about this client. Is she a VIP?"

He stops suddenly, face to face with an enormous, heavily muscled man dressed in dark sunglasses and head-to-toe black.

"I guess that answers my question," Blake mutters, then smiles up at the guy. At least 6'5", the man dominates the room. "Unless you're the one getting the makeover, sir."

"I am the princess's bodyguard," he says in a commanding monotone. "Who are you?"

Blake turns to Olivia. "Too bad I forgot my suspenders," he says. "This feels like a really special occasion."

***

After convincing the bodyguard Olivia is supposed to be there, and Blake is a real journalist, as opposed to someone from a true gossip network like TMZ, he finally allows them to pass. The relief is only momentary, though—they are greeted to a fresh round of chaos.

Guess there's no limit on daily dramas, at least in the Harper James Salon world.

Scattered around the space are a dozen other bodyguards, also dressed in black and just as intimidating. Some stand in place, like statues, while others circle the room, like great whites, looking intense and speaking quietly into earpieces. Ursula isn't around, thank the lord, but plenty of others are. There's Gia and Glory, standing in the doorframe of the break room hallway, watching the scene with stunned expressions; across the room, the C's do the same, only they look more excited than anything.

"This is a place of business, and you have no right!"

Not surprisingly, only Zoe refuses to hide. She stands at the center of the room, looking up at one of the men with defiant annoyance. "This is an invasion of privacy," she barks, and it is an arresting sight—Zoe, with her bright blond hair, pale pink mohair sweater and skinny pale pink stretch cotton pants, glaring up at a scary-looking, black-clad man twice her size. "You can't just come storming in here, do you understand me? You can give me that look all you want, too . . . I will not be intimidated, do you understand? I've already called security and they'll be here any second."

Olivia realizes she's just been standing there, watching. Like this is some scene from a movie that has nothing to do with her. "Wait, that's not necessary," she says, rushing over. "They're here for *my* client."

"You!" Zoe spins around, directing her fury in an entirely new direction. "I should have known this distraction was all your fault!"

"Hey, I didn't know about this! It's for Jasmin's client! She's a royal, but I had no idea these . . ."

"Oh, Abdu. Must you? Please stand back and relax." The voice is curt and crisp, ringing through the room. Everyone freezes, turning to see . . . a tall, enthralling woman. Instantly, Olivia knows she is the kind of person who commands attention, and not just due to her royal status, or even her attire. Covered in layers of plum fabric, the only glimpse of flesh are her hands and face, which stares out from an intricately wrapped hijab, also in deep purple. Gold metallic thread accents throughout the fabric. Regal. Yet, even with such extensive concealment, one fact is undeniable: this woman is utterly gorgeous. High cheekbones, skin the color of a caramel mochaccino, and wide-set brown eyes with flecks of gold, accentuated by the metallic thread. Princess or not, she's the kind of woman for whom people stop and stare, momentarily mesmerized.

Zoe, for example, whose mouth is hanging open.

"I mean, really, Abdu." She gives an audible sigh. "Is this entirely necessary?"

"It's for your safety, my Highness," says the security guard who had been arguing with Zoe. "We have orders to clear and sweep any room."

"How exhausting," she says, then suddenly smiles, lighting up the room. "But we have arrived, at the very least! Now, who is . . . no, wait!" she says giddily, clapping her hands. "Don't tell me! I love a guessing game!" She scans the room, faintly amused, eyes passing from Glory to Gia to the C's. "No," she mutters to herself, "No, no . . ." She stops for a second on Zoe, who, in the face of an actual Royal, has undergone an attitude shift, trading her dour expression for her most winning cosmetically altered white smile. "Your Highness, it's so lovely to be in your presence."

"Absolutely not," says the Princess, giving a slight grimace towards Zoe as she moves on. Then she stops suddenly, beaming, her eyes focused on another person.

"You must be Olivia," she says. "I just knew."

A deep breath and Olivia walks forward. "Your Highness," she says somberly. "I am honored to aid in choosing your attire today." Then, as silly as she feels, Olivia puts a leg behind her and gives a deep, elegant curtsy, her head bowed.

Glad I forced Gwynnie to take those etiquette classes, she thinks. She had hated them, but at least had learned something.

She rises, and the Princess gives a nod and benevolent smile. "The pleasure is mine, Olivia."

"Excuse me, I don't mean to be rude or anything," says Zoe. *Why stop now?* "I realize our VIP clients have special requirements, but this really has been an imposition. We should have been given notice, and where is *our* security? They need to approve these kinds of things."

"They just did," says the Princess's guard. "I've been informed."

"By what, telepathy?" questions Zoe.

"Earpiece. But ask them yourself, if you are so inclined."

He motions to the door, where several members of the Harper James security staff have appeared, as well as one of Olivia's most detested people—the ever-present Nazi HR unibrow-uniboob, herself. And at the very front, as polished as ever and wearing a nonchalant expression.

Marcus Courtney.

Zoe immediately rushes over. "I'm so glad you're here," she says to him, looking up at him as though greeting a heroic knight coming to save her from a burning village. "This has been incredibly inconvenient for the Salon. For you."

"Yes, I understand," says Marcus. He's already headed towards the center of the room, leaving Zoe aghast. "Your Highness," he says to the princess. "Marcus Courtney, I oversee high-level clientele."

This is news to Olivia. The Princess takes it in stride, offering a bemused smile. "I'm terribly sorry for any mix-up," he tells her. "We weren't aware of your visit . . . I was just informed. But we couldn't be more pleased. Let me be the first to officially welcome you to the Harper James Salon, and please tell me if there is anything at all I can do to make your visit as pleasant and seamless as possible."

"It is rather chaotic," she says. "I am not used to such crowds."

"That will be taken care of immediately. All Salon associates will be clearing the space for the remainder of your visit," he says, eyes circling the room with a knowing look.

"Wait," says Zoe, flabbergasted. "What about *our* clients?"

"All appointments will be rescheduled," he says, giving her a pointed look. He turns back to the Princess with a charming grin. "Except for Olivia, that is. I've spoken with your security staff and understand the need for discretion. The room will be cleared momentarily, allowing for privacy during the duration of your stay." The Princess nods, satisfied. "And let me say again, what an honor to have you, your Highness. Please think of the Harper James Salon as your second home."

***

Once the order has been given, everything swings into action. The women quickly gather their purses and coats, exiting the room—even Zoe does not argue, though she's seething with every step. Once the room is empty, the Princess gives a slight wave, and the security team disappears to the lobby to await further orders. "Anything else I can do for you now, Princess Nayef?" says the Head of Security.

"That'll be all," she tells him. "Just close the door behind you."

Suddenly, they are alone, the Salon vast and silent around them. Then a sound breaks the air—laughter. Peals of them.

"I owe Jasmin a hundred bucks," says the Princess, wiping tears from her eyes. "I mean, that curtsey! Don't get me wrong, it was great. Very elegant. But a curtsey! I told her, no way, she won't do it . . . but I was totally wrong!"

"I don't understand, Princess?"

"Forget that princess stuff, call me Noura."

"But isn't the formality proper etiquette?"

"Don't get me wrong, I'm second level royal . . . but first level princess? No need for any formal anything." She wiggles, uncomfortably. "Lord, I've got to get out of these clothes too . . . so uncomfortable. My mom would love it, but seriously, it's like carrying an extra twenty pounds." She reaches around, attempting to unwrap the layer. "May I help?" asks Olivia, to which she nods. In no time, she has been unwrapped, revealing a long black tunic and wide-legged navy pants, (Coco Chanel was the first to pair black with navy) still offering full coverage, but undeniable sophistication. "Obviously, Harper James is not in tune with the modest fashion craze . . . but Jasmin finds a way to get me great stuff. She picked this outfit. Not the hijabs, though Neiman's has a full line of luxury ones now." She adjusts her head wrap. "You like it?"

"Yes, it's lovely."

"Modern Saudi women need not dress like their great-grandmothers, but I suppose not everyone got the memo. To tell you the truth, I wouldn't have given this place the time of day without Jasmin. I'm glad she's getting out of here."

Olivia is beginning to understand.

"So, this was all . . . an act?"

"You could call it that, I suppose. And wasn't I great?" She starts laughing again. "Can hardly believe we pulled it off so fast."

"The security guards too?"

"I usually have one on hand, but I demand they stay incognito. My father insists on the protection, especially when I travel abroad. Personally, I hate all that pomp and circumstance—I prefer a low profile. That said, on the off chance of an emergency, we have a full team on 24/7 call." She grins. "This wasn't the kind of emergency they are trained for, but they know not to question my orders. Even when I told them to play up the menacing factor. And everyone fell for it right away . . . even that man . . . what was his name? Mark?"

"Marcus."

"Marcus. Handsome, but what a sucker. A few guys in sunglasses, the word princess, and he's clearing the joint."

Olivia shakes her head, now laughing too. "So, Jasmin did all this? I can't believe she pulled it off so quickly and so easily."

"It wasn't just for you, Olivia. It was her grand finale F-you. Excuse my language, but she hates this place, and has since she started. I'm so pleased she's relocating. I only came here for her."

"Here? You've been here before?"

She raises her eyebrows. "Many times. Of course, I wasn't wearing all that, just the head scarf . . . but it was me, Noura. No one bothered to pay much attention, you see. So much for a mecca of personalized service, of customer care. Incognito, fine, but I'm practically invisible to the women who work here. Jasmin says you are different, though . . . that you aren't an idiot like the rest. That you have a great sense of style, is it true?"

"Well, I . . ."

"No, don't answer that. Just show me. For all this effort, that's the least I deserve!" Then she stops suddenly. "Wait, I forgot something. The reporter. Jasmin mentioned he'd be here."

"Oh my God!" says Olivia. "I forgot too! He's probably out in the lobby with the security guys . . ."

"Well, what are you waiting for? Fetch him. I don't mind playing the princess card a bit longer, if you can excuse a little more hoity-toity self-entitlement."

"Of course!" says Olivia. "The more the better."

"Good. Funny, I quite enjoy the humor of the uppity façade," she giggles, then winks. "Especially the curtsey part."

***

Once he is ushered back in, Blake seems nonplussed by the turn of events, if not intrigued. As for Noura, she seamlessly morphs back into princess role, making demands of Olivia and offering verdicts on each garment selection from Jasmin's rolling rack. Olivia plays along, deferring to her every option, while offering up honest options and potential pairings. *Perhaps that blouse is better suited to the Chanel pants, your Royal Highness? I believe a statement necklace would be the perfect accessory, if your Royal Highness might indulge me and try one on?*

Several times, Noura almost breaks character, turning away so Blake won't see her laugh. But ultimately, they pull off the act, and the final sale is significant. More than significant, even. "Yes, all of that," says Noura, pointing out the items she wants. "Have a bill sent to us at the Four Seasons. The items can also be delivered to our private hotel concierge." From his unobtrusive perch on a stool in the corner, even Blake looks impressed.

At the Salon door, Noura bids Olivia goodbye. "I hope your needs have been met," says Olivia.

"I am very pleased," she says. "Jasmin told me you are skilled, and she was correct. It was lovely to meet you, Olivia."

"You as well," says Olivia. Then, bowing her head in respect—and to hide her grin—she drops into a low, regal curtsey. One so on point it would make the Windsors of Kensington Palace blush.

"Excellent. Now, I really must go," says Noura, then disappears into the lobby. Even behind the closed door, Olivia can swear she hears a giggle.

Olivia stands, still overwhelmed.

"Well, one thing is for sure," says Blake. "This place is full of surprises."

"You don't know the half of it," she says, heading over to straighten Jasmin's dressing room.

"But I think I have enough for my article," deems Blake.

Olivia turns to him, feeling a strange disappointment. "You're done, then?"

"I think so. And I've got to say, Olivia . . . you've been a great host."

"I'd say the same about you, but . . . guess I better read the article first."

They smile at each other, and Olivia knows she should be relieved. Finally, back to normal—or slightly less insane, at the least. Things won't be normal at the Salon, Olivia has come to terms with that, and the environment will be even more dysfunctional after today. Her outcast status fully cemented, resentment at an all-time high—still, there won't be a reporter there to chronicle it, so that's something.

Olivia should be relieved. Yet the idea of not seeing Blake again makes her feel strangely hollow, even sad.

"I might need some final quotes, maybe," he says, gazing off into space.

"Sure. Any time."

"Maybe we could meet again . . . I mean, just for some final questions." Hearing the request, Olivia feels unexpected tingles in her gut.

"Sure thing. As long as the meeting involves coffee."

A flush of relief, a slow, wide grin. "Sounds great," he says, heading towards the door. "Oh, and Olivia?"

"Yes?"

"You're really great at this job."

"Thanks," she says, watching him leave. And only then, left alone in that massive space, does the reality set in. After all the obstacles, she pushed through. Despite the manipulation and stumbling blocks, the sabotage and backstabbing, she made her clients look good. She made them happy and cemented relationships. Still, she was completely spent and numb from the day's insanity.

Chapter Five

The next morning, Olivia wakes up still in shock. *Did all that really happen?* She lies in bed, staring at the ceiling and going over the events of the previous day quickly in her head, right until she arrived home to a waiting Gwynnie and Gladys.

Olivia sits up, a smile on her face. That might have been the best part of all.

Olivia left soon after Blake had, exhausted, and wary of facing any returning Salon employees. She thought about calling her mother and filling her in but decided to wait. Better to tell her in person, she'd thought, rushing to catch an early train. *I can't wait to see her face.*

She needn't wait long—the second she opened the door, there were her mother and Gwynnie, ready and waiting. They turned to her, faces eager. "So?" Gladys had said, not even offering a hello. "What happened? Go on, tell us . . . hurry up, please? We've been waiting!"

"Can I take off my coat first?" asked Olivia.

"No," said Gladys. "Sit down and spill it."

Olivia had done as told, giving them a play by play, not leaving out a single detail. She'd told them about meeting Blake that morning, and the surprise awaiting them in the Salon. "You've got to be kidding me!" Gladys had exclaimed. "That little bitch stole your client?"

"Yes. Zoe." Olivia had corrected.

"I'll rip her evil little head off, whatever her stupid name is."

She'd gone on to explain about Jasmin's intervention, the substitute client and the scene that awaited them upstairs. "Wait, so she isn't a princess?"

"She's a second level royal, or something like that, but doesn't act like it. It was all for show."

"So cool," Gwynnie had said. "Go on, Mom."

She ended by speaking of the huge sale and Blake's compliment. "Of course, you're good at your job, an idiot could see that," Gladys had responded—though she'd left out the part where he suggested they meet again. Maybe it wasn't anything but what he'd said . . . *a follow-up interview*. Still, Olivia can't help but feel a little excited at the prospect of seeing him again.

Olivia finishes the story, and for a second, Gladys and Gwynnie had been silent. Then, like an explosion, Gwynnie had jumped to her feet, throwing her arms around Olivia. "I knew you could do it Mom! You're such a badass!"

"Language," said Gladys, then gave a smug smile. "Well, I for one, am not surprised," she'd said. "I knew today would go well, so I planned a celebration dinner. My famous Hadassah Sisterhood apricot preserve glazed roasted chicken recipe will be ready in twenty."

***

The next morning, Gladys is still basking in the glow of her daughter's success. "Things will be different now, Olivia," she said, forcing her to wait for a piece of toast. "The point has been made. You are a force to be reckoned with! Mark my words, those girls will keep their distance from here on out. Butter? Jam?"

"You think? Seriously? Just butter, please."

"I know," she'd said, forcing the buttered toast in her hand, followed by a to-go cup of freshly squeezed orange juice. "Now hurry up, you don't want to miss the train. And don't forget to reapply your lipstick when you're done. All eyes will be on you, as they should. You need to look perfect." She smiles, pride in her eyes. "I knew you could do it, sweetheart. This is the beginning of a new era for you."

***

The extra boost of confidence was all Olivia needed. On her walk from the train to Harper James, she applied her lipstick in a beautiful shade of Sephora private label peony pink as any last-minute concerns seemed to float away. *What could they do to her now?* She'd not only rebounded from Zoe's attempted sabotage but done it in a big way. So big, Marcus even stepped in to help. Olivia, the new girl, brought in the highest caliber of client—with Jasmin's help, for sure, and Noura's willingness to act the part—and showed everyone what they were dealing with. Despite all the obstacles, she'd come out ahead, proving herself to everyone. Including a reporter who maybe, just maybe, had kinda-sorta asked her out on a pseudo date.

Striding into Harper James, she sees a familiar uniform ahead—Willard, his back turned. *Oh my God*, she thinks. *Marguerite! And Daphne!* In all her excitement, she forgot to call and fill them in. Now that it had all worked out, she wanted to tell them everything . . . but she'd been so overwhelmed and exhausted the night before. *I'll tell Willard that Marguerite should expect a call*, she thinks, heading towards the security guard. *She will hardly believe everything!* She then thinks, *ok, I will call Daphne in the next day or two after I catch my breath.*

"Willard!" she says, and the man turns. Only he isn't Willard at all. Same height and closely cropped graying hair, but the face is much younger and wears a confused expression.

"How may I help you?"

"Sorry, it was the uniform . . . I thought you were the head of security."

"I am."

"But Willard . . ."

"Oh, Mr. Smith? He's not here anymore. But maybe I can help you?"

"Wait," says Olivia, confused. "Where did he go?"

"I have no idea," says the man. "I just started yesterday." He extends a hand. "Ralph Langton. I'll be overseeing Harper James security from here on out. And you are . . . ?"

"Olivia Kopelman," she says, giving him a quick shake. "But . . . sorry, I have to go. I'm late."

She turns before he can respond, heading towards the elevator with a sudden heaviness in her chest. No way he was fired, not with his son. *His pension must have kicked in*, Olivia reasons, as the elevator arrives, and she steps in. *But why didn't he say goodbye, at least?*

Things change, Olivia tells herself, watching the floor numbers light up as they rise. *That's just how it is.* And in a weird way, things worked out perfectly. *Onward and upward*, she thinks. She imagines her new world at Harper James, trusting that this job will continue to deliver the security and new future she so desperately needs.

Immediately, something feels unfamiliar. Usually, the Salon is buzzing with energy, but today is different. She scans the room. Ursula is in the corner of her dressing room, quietly sorting garments, back turned. A few feet away, Gia holds the phone close, whispering to whomever is on the other end.

Olivia hadn't expected a warm reception, not by any means. The silent treatment, even. But dead silence, not so much. She releases the door, and it closes behind her with a thud, the sound echoing through the empty space. Ursula and Gia look up, spotting her, then turn away just as quickly.

What's going on? Where is everyone? Jasmin is gone, obviously, and Glory is probably hidden back in her room. But what about the C-Cups and Zoe? Between Willard's sudden exit, and now them, Olivia has a strange feeling. She opens her mouth to ask Ursula and Gia what's going on, then stops suddenly. Something about the way Gia glanced away, and how their bodies are turned from her, tell her to stay away.

What now?

Enough of this, thinks Olivia. No more surprises, no more fashion espionage ploys. Enough with the games and secrecy, she thinks, legs already moving towards the break room hallway. After everything that has happened, I deserve to know what's going on.

Glory, thinks Olivia, heading for her door. A knock—no answer. A louder one, but nothing. She turns the knob, but the door won't open. Olivia steps back, confused. Glory never locks this door. Olivia didn't even know it *could* lock.

What the fuck is going on?

That's when she hears the whispering. Instantly, Olivia is headed towards the source. The break room door is also shut. Or almost—the tiniest bit ajar, just enough for a spec of light and whispers to carry through. Without making the decision, Olivia storms over, raptly pushing it open wide.

Three faces turn upwards, looking directly at her. Zoe and the C's, gathered in their favorite gossip spot around the table. Only this time, there are no untouched diet and sugar-free, gluten-free muffins or green juice, no giddy expressions that usually accompany their cruel critiques. The C-Cups stare at her with wide eyes, looking nervous and unnerved.

Only Zoe looks unsurprised, gazing up at Olivia with a placid calmness.

"Oh, hello Olivia," she says.

"What's going on, Zoe?" she says, stepping into the room.

"I don't think I'm the right person to answer that," Zoe says. Then, as if in slow motion, all three heads turn to the left, Olivia following their gaze.

They are not alone. There is a fourth figure, obscured by the door. Mug in hand, she leans against the counter, immediately recognizable.

Olivia would know that uniboob and unibrow anywhere. Carol Ann, the nasty HR, Third Reich, miserable troll.

"Oh, Olivia," she says, jumping to attention. "You're here."

"Where else might I be?"

"Exactly my point," she says, stepping forward. "If you wouldn't mind, please gather your things and follow me upstairs."

"Why?" The word comes out louder than expected, giving Carol Ann a start.

"We can discuss that on the way," she says. "I'm on strict orders to accompany you upstairs."

"Wait . . . can I at least stop at my desk? Take off my coat?"

"I'm sorry, but you cannot." Carol Ann steps past her, into the hallway.

"I need to check my messages. See if any clients have called."

"Olivia, I'm under strict orders. We need to go upstairs immediately."

Olivia is more confused than before, but also suddenly aware. Aware of Zoe and the C's watching her every move, relishing in her discomfort.

"Fine," says Olivia. She has no idea what this is about, but she won't give them the pleasure. "Lead the way."

It feels like an eternity, following the woman down the break room hallway, then making the long trek through the Salon. It's like being called to the principal's office, only as an adult, and the principal holds your entire financial livelihood and sense of self-worth in his hand; Olivia is in trouble, but she has no idea why, or what she may have done.

Don't let them see how nervous you are, she tells herself, lifting her head high. Stare straight ahead and don't think of looking back.

At the lobby door, Carol Ann holds it open. "After you," she says. That's when Olivia makes her mistake.

Just the quickest glance behind as she steps through—only a split-second, but that's enough. Enough to see Gia and Ursula watching with thinly veiled fascination, and the three girls clustered in the hallway door frame, making no attempt to hide anything. Zoe, Chrissy and Catie, watching her, their faces lit up with utter glee.

After a silent elevator ride, they exited on a familiar floor, but hardly the Lido Deck. Upper management. "Follow me," says Carol, heading towards HR. Only instead of stopping, she forges ahead. Olivia's heart drops. Once she sees Felix's office up ahead, she's totally confused. "Carol Ann! What's going on? I don't understand! Have I done something wrong?" Whatever is going on, the second she spots Felix, Olivia knows that he'll intervene.

No luck. His door is closed and . . . wait. *Isn't this his door?* Olivia is sure it is, yet the gold plate with his name has disappeared, only a faint square outline remaining.

Oh, fuck.

Now they are nearing the end of the hall, a place where Olivia has never been, nor longed to go. The hidden depths of Harper James management, the mysterious inner workings—like Oz behind the big obscure curtain, this is the place where big decisions are made.

Next to an open door, Carol Ann stops suddenly. "Here we are," she says.

Great, thinks Olivia. *Where, exactly, is that? And why am I here?* Carol Ann motions for her to enter, and Olivia does not hesitate or pause. Whatever this is, she wants to hurry it up to an immediate ending.

The room is bright, floor to ceiling windows letting in the natural sunlight. There's a long, polished wood table, bodies lining each side. A half dozen or so—one woman, and the rest men. Beyond the woman who sits pin straight, contemplating her notes, the others have made themselves comfortable . . . sipping and slurping their coffee, eating pastries like cave animals from a silver tray at the center of the table, chatting amongst themselves. Far from the great D.C. dinner party scenes of Olivia's past. No one looks familiar, but it is hard to tell—in her discomfort and confusion, they seem to meld together into one solitary figure—Corporate White Guy. With shiny hair, gym-toned body and designer suit; Corporate White Guy, biting into a croissant, probably boasting about his golf game and reveling in the confidence that comes from a high-powered job, full health care, a paid off mortgage and healthy stock options.

And there, smack in front of them yet utterly invisible: Olivia.

"Olivia Kopelman," announces Carol Ann, and instantly the faces rotate, turning her visible once again.

"Thank you for joining us, Olivia," says a deep, yet familiar voice at the end of the table. The man rises, distinguishing himself from the others. "How are you today?" Olivia tries not to show her utter shock.

"Fine, Marcus. Thank you."

"Won't you take a seat?"

"I will," she says, noting the sole empty one in front of her. "I take it this one's for me."

She lowers herself into the chair, aware the men have already made their initial assessments—she knows men like these quite well. Those years with Edwin, she met more than she can count. She knows how quickly they analyze, access, reach a conclusion– by now, they've taken stock of her every inch, from the way she stands to the firmness of her ass. They've noted the way she responds, without hesitation, as well as her use of Marcus's first name. They've taken in the data, processed it quickly and come to their initial conclusions: ball-buster or bitch, sex-kitten or pliant. Or maybe, judging by the stifled yawn on the left, just plain boring.

She also knows how little it matters. Whatever their feelings, or beliefs or thoughts, her fate was determined long before she set foot in the room. Only, for all her insight, that part is still a blank. What that determination might be, and how it came to exist in the first place.

"So," he says, returning to his seat at the head of the table. "You are probably wondering why we called you in today," says Marcus.

No shit. "Yes. I am curious."

"First, would you like a beverage?" asks Marcus, oozing with professionalism, all his natural flirtations seeming to have evaporated away. "Coffee? Tea?"

"I'd rather know why I'm here."

"Straight to the point," he says. "I respect your being forthcoming, so let us offer the same." He turns to his left, where the serious looking woman sits. "This is Ruthie Barratta, the Senior VP of HR."

Senior VP of HR? Wasn't that . . . Olivia glances behind her, Carol Ann is gone.

"Recently appointed Senior VP of HR," clarifies Marcus.

"That's right," says the woman, jumping in. "Hello, Miss Kopelman. Thank you for joining us today."

Olivia nods. *As if I had a choice, bitch.* She thinks.

The woman glances down at her yellow legal pad of paper, and Olivia notes her severe pageboy haircut (hair a mousey brown color) and makeup-less face (has she even heard of powder?), her skin tinged the same gray as her ill-fitting and second-rate business pant suit. This may be an iconic fashion institution, but between Ruthie's ultimate drabness and Carol Ann's uni-everything, Olivia wonders when HR will get the memo.

"You must be wondering why you are here," Ruthie says. "So, let me put it to you bluntly: in recent days, Harper James has undergone a transition. A house cleaning, in layman's terms."

Willard, thinks Olivia. *Please tell me he left by choice.*

"We take that responsibility seriously, which is why we convened this expert advisory board to aid in the process." Around the table, a few nods and self-satisfied grunts from the so-called expert crowd. "We've had to make some tough decisions regarding several departments, including the Salon."

"Are you closing us down?" asks Olivia, the words just popping out.

"No. Downsizing."

"Rightsizing," says Olivia, almost to herself.

"Well . . . yes," says Marcus, taken aback. "That's it exactly."

They couldn't mean . . . .*no way.* Olivia glances at Marcus, but he's looking away. *Shit, this can't be happening. This can't . . .*

"I'm sure you'll understand, Olivia," Ruthie continues. "We've had to make some difficult decisions."

Olivia won't let this happen. Not after everything. Not after how far she's come.

"Wait a second," says Olivia. "Before you go on, let me just say something."

"That's not necessary, Olivia."

"I'll be brief, I promise." Then, before Ruthie can stop her, Olivia jumps in. She talks quickly, listing off her accomplishments, appealing to reason. She's been there a short time, she explains. But her sales numbers, her caliber of clients, her growth . . .

"Enough," says Ruthie, stopping her cold. "We are well aware of your successes, Olivia."

"So . . . you're letting me go?"

Ruthie sighs. "It isn't always about numbers. We hold our employees to high standards, Olivia. And while your sales have been good, there are some aspects of your tenure that cannot be overlooked."

"What aspects?"

"We've been made aware of several policy violations, the seriousness of which necessitated the convening of this Board."

"Policy violations?" says Olivia, shocked. "What do you mean?"

"Is this really necessary?" says Ruthie. "I'd rather not embarrass you more than necessary."

"I think we're past that by now, Ruthie," says Olivia, leaning in. "Tell me. How, exactly, did I violate policy?"

Ruth sighs. "If you really want to know . . ."

"Of course, I do! This is outrageous!"

"Fine," she says, reaching for a remote. "Why don't I show you instead?" She clicks a button and a curtain lifts on the wall, revealing a flat screen monitor. Another click and the room lights dim.

Suddenly, a flash of light, and an image bursts on the screen . . . footage. Albeit grainy, taken from a security camera, but the locale is unmistakable.

The breakroom. Someone pacing in a circle, clutching something in her hands, obviously distressed. She knows the figure right away.

It is herself, Olivia.

"There are several issues at play," says Ruthie. "The behavioral ones being key."

"Wait," says Olivia. "There are cameras in there? I don't understand. When was this taken? I don't remember any cameras."

Olivia stops suddenly, knowing exactly when this was taken, and exactly what will come next. She tightens her fists under the table, eyes fixed to the small version of herself projected onto the screen.

Oh, no, thinks Olivia, too dumbstruck to speak, frozen in place as the grainy version of her races towards the sink in a frenzied burst. She is turned away now, looking like a crazy person. Arms moving frantically, back falling and rising in rhythm. You don't have to see her face to know she is hysterical, sobbing.

"You've had sudden outbursts," says Ruthie, in the monotone voice of one narrating a nature documentary. "Displayed aggressive behavior."

As if on cue, the figure on the screen launches something at the wall . . ."

The stained white pants.

"Exhibited unpredictable behaviors," says Ruthie. Olivia watches, cringing, as the screen version of herself launches forward, kicking bags.

"Wait," says Olivia. "There's more to that . . . look, I was trying to get out a stain and it just . . . it was a bad day. One bad day! It isn't representative of some larger issue!"

"There are additional issues as well," says Ruthie. "The lapses in morality."

"Morality?" spits Olivia, fighting the urge to launch herself forward, slide across the wood and ring Ruthie's scrawny neck. "Why would you question . . . my morality?"

Instead of answering, there's another click. Instantly, the footage is gone, replaced by a new locale. The front door of Harpers, leading onto 5th Avenue. The door opens, a figure racing through. Hunched over, hurrying, arms heavy with bags.

Click. Ruthie pauses the footage.

"That's you, Olivia. Correct?"

"I . . ."

"And what do you have in those bags?"

"Merchandise, but I . . ."

Shit. She'd forgotten. In all the craziness, it was still there. "I returned it, obviously! I mean, everyone knows I brought it all right back in! I placed it all along the wall next to cosmetics. Your camera must have also caught that footage! I'd be an idiot to try and steal . . ."

"You shouldn't have taken it in the first place. A sudden ethical revelation does not erase the fact."

"It wasn't mine, it belonged to a client! And I didn't take it! I was upset and didn't realize I was still carrying everything. And I would have . . ." says Olivia, voice rising.

"Exactly, it wasn't yours. Yet you took it anyway."

"But I brought it all right back in when I realized I was still carrying the bags!" shouts Olivia.

"The footage speaks for itself."

"Wait a second, that's not . . . this isn't fair! It's all taken out of context, out of . . . you guys don't understand. You aren't listening!"

"We are, Olivia. But your words are unnecessary. The images say everything."

Click.

The lights come on in a sudden burst, momentarily blinding Olivia. She blinks, trying to clear the blurriness, and feels wetness run down her cheeks . . . oh shit . . . *is she crying?*

And when did she get on her feet?

Olivia takes a deep breath, trying to focus herself. Slowly, the room around her comes into view. The table, full of faces—all carefully turned away, so as not to embarrass her. Not to embarrass the woman in front of them—the one who has risen to her feet, tears running down her cheeks.

"I know what you all must be thinking," she says, fighting to keep her voice level. "But this is a misunderstanding, all of it. What you saw on that footage was taken out of context, misconstrued. That's why I'm upset. Not because I'm . . . *unhinged.*" She circles the room with her eyes, desperate for something—a moment of understanding, a sign she is being heard. But every time she catches an eye, it darts away just as quickly. She forces herself to sit and take another breath. *Be calm*, Olivia tells herself. *Be rational.*

"Look, I apologize for this outburst," she says. "I'm emotional because . . . I love this job. And I'm good at it. I'm a professional. What you saw up there, well . . . that's not me. You took it out of context."

"But it was you," says Ruthie softly, with almost a tinge of compassion. "That was exactly who we saw on footage."

"But it isn't indicative of . . ." She stops suddenly. "Wait . . . the footage. That's it! You just need to see more footage. Right before that part in the break room. If you see what came before, you'll understand." She looks at Ruthie, hopeful. "I just need to find Willard. His son, Devon, can pull the tape and show you exactly what happened."

"That's not possible, Olivia. Devon is gone, and so is the footage."

"Gone? You mean he was fired?"

"I cannot speak further on this."

"And the footage?"

"Enough, Olivia. Unfortunately, we are going in circles."

"But Willard . . . wait. You fired him, right? And Devon went with him."

Ruthie sighs. "These are private personnel matters." She looks around the table, sensing the room around her growing more uncomfortable. The men shift in their seat, one clears his throat. Another coughs.

Why are they all here? Thinks Olivia. All these people for one . . . rightsizing? She suddenly remembers something, glancing down the table. The leader, at the head of the table—only he's been silent, unobtrusive. He's been so nonexistent Olivia had almost forgotten he was there.

"I have just one more question," says Olivia. She turns her gaze directly ahead, right at Marcus. "For Felix."

"I think we've reached an impasse, Olivia," says Ruthie, rising. "But, please, know we appreciate your coming in today. Now, why don't we have Security escort you upstairs to collect your things."

"Security? Are you kidding me? Nope," says Olivia. "Not so quick."

"Excuse me?" says Ruthie. Olivia ignores her, gazing in another direction. "Marcus. Where is Felix? I need to speak with him."

Marcus breaks eye contact, looking at the ceiling instead. "I think this has gone far enough, Olivia." But it's too late. In the split-second before he looked away, she got her answer.

Felix is gone, right along with Willard and Devon. And in their place? A new Advisory Committee, and a new leader at the head of the table. It's everything Felix feared come to life; this isn't a Harper James overhaul, it's a coup.

This meeting had been an excuse, a façade . . . Olivia had to go, and they needed an excuse. Her numbers were the highest in the Salon, and her client list quickly became the most impressive. So, without real reasons for letting her go, they'd cobbled one together—edited it, really, out of random footage.

The revelation comes to Olivia with startling clarity. Another set-up, just like all the others, only this one intended to be her final nail in the Harper James Salon's coffin. But still, staring at Marcus, one question haunts her.

Why?

Since this is her big exit, might as well ask the source. *It's not like I have anything else to lose*, she thinks, glaring at Marcus. He shifts in his chair, growing visibly uncomfortable.

"Good job with the footage, Marcus. Smart move. I mean, with that kind of behavior, what other choice do you have but to fire me? But here's the part I don't quite get . . . why fire me at all?"

"Olivia," he says, standing. "I realize you're upset, but this has gotten out of hand."

"I'm not upset, Marcus. I just want a little clarity. I mean, it isn't the quality of my work . . . I'm good at this job, and you know it. So . . . was it, Felix? He discovered me, after all. Mentored me. Maybe you figured it wasn't enough to get rid of him, but everything associated with him as well. Particularly, me."

"Olivia, this has gone far enough."

"But that doesn't make sense, not really." He glances around the table apologetically, smiling good-naturedly. *Isn't this unfortunate?* His expression seems to say. *That we must deal with occasional unhinged employees?*

"Yeah, and that's another thing . . . why the audience? I mean, if you're the big Harper James boss, why would you need an audience to let go of little old me? Sure, it's great back up, just in case. They can always step in and affirm just how nuts I am." She circles the table with her eyes. "I'm crazy, right guys? A total freakin' nut case."

"Well, if the designer shoe fits," says Marcus, trying to keep his voice light. Only the joke falls flat. Everyone just stares at him, then back at Olivia, too mesmerized to stop the show.

"Or if, say, I wanted to sue. Say it was unfair, my firing. Well, you've got six perfectly levelheaded men—oh, and one woman! Sorry, Ruthie! To say just how unstable I really was, in case of, I don't know, a suit for unlawful termination."

Now, Marcus is standing, motioning Ruthie towards the door. *Security*, he mouths, as if Olivia isn't right in front of him, watching his lips move. Olivia watches the woman scurry towards the door, once again struck by how dumpy she looks. *Seriously, this is Harper James... can't they do an employee makeover day? Consider it community service, even, just don't make that poor woman go another second with a bowl mouse brown haircut and gray skin, it's just cruel. Is she wearing gray lipstick?*

"Or wait!" says Olivia, another possibility jumping into her head. "Maybe that wasn't the kind of lawsuit that worried you! Maybe it was another variety." She looks around the table. "The kind you guys hate worst of all."

She mouths just as slowly and obviously as Marcus did moments before.

Sexual Harassment.

"Why do you look so shocked?" she asks him. "Was I wrong? That isn't it? Well, my bad. I guess this isn't about a potential sexual harassment lawsuit either. So, what's left? I'm at a loss. There's only one other reason you could possibly have fired me, I suppose. But it couldn't be that, could it? I'm almost too embarrassed to say." In the hallway behind her, Olivia hears footsteps approaching, stomping closer by the second.

"Okay, I'll say it," Olivia tells him calmly, just as the security men appear. "It's because I said no, right?"

"Miss," says one of the men. "Miss, we're going to have to ask you to follow us."

"I mean, no way you fired me," she says calmly. "Because I wouldn't suck your skinny little pencil dick."

That's the final straw. "How dare you!" bellows Marcus, his face bright red. "How dare you insinuate something so ridiculous."

"Okay, I'm ready," says Olivia, looking up at the security guard with a pleasant smile. "Lead the way."

***

Out by the elevator, Olivia turns to Ruthie. "I need to get my stuff from the Salon," she says, suddenly, strangely calm. "Since I won't be returning, I assume."

"We can have it sent to you."

"My day planner, coat . . . my purse is up there. Unless you plan on paying for my transportation home, I need five minutes." *Not to mention my cell phone*, Olivia thinks. The last thing I need is those bitches having access to everyone on my contact list. Who knows what they might do? "Come on, Ruthie. Look, I'm completely calm. Just let me get my stuff and go." She glances at the security men. "These guys can even come along."

Sure, Zoe will see them, the C-Cups too. But what does it matter anymore? Who cares what those girls think, and besides . . . she doesn't work at the infamous Salon. Anymore.

It doesn't seem real, she thinks. Neither does the chaotic scene she just exited. Shock, maybe? Or more likely, Olivia has just had enough.

"Fine," says Ruthie, looking exasperated. "But make it quick."

"Sounds great," says Olivia, pushing the elevator button up. "Like the most fucked-up field trip of all time."

Olivia can't be sure, but she swears Ruthie stifles a laugh.

***

In and out, that's how it will go. She'll be laser-focused, make a b-line for her stuff—coat, phone, purse, *check, check check*—then head straight for the door leading out, never to look back. Thirty seconds top, that's the plan.

At least, the plan in her head. The one she recites to herself like a mantra on the silent ride up the elevator, blocking out the fact she is sandwiched between two security guards and to her left, Ruthie from HR, who watches her with eyes to kill. Like poison darts.

It is all too much. She's still in shock, and only one thing is clear—the quicker Olivia escapes this dark fashion hellhole, the better chances of her long-term survival.

In and out. Thirty seconds flat.

She makes it. Almost.

In the Salon lobby, she turns to the guards. "Can you wait out here?" she asks. "I swear I'll be fast."

The guards look at each other, then the bigger one shrugs. "Fine, but you better make this quick. And you are not allowed to take anything out of the store with any logo or connection to Harper James. Including your client book."

Not a problem, thinks Olivia. Keep your fucking client book. It's more like *Schindler's List* to me now, anyway. She's never wanted anything more than to exit this place. She swings open the lobby door and takes a big, deep breath. *Go*, she tells herself, and hightails it inside.

She doesn't run or even speed walk—just a quick stride, eyes focused on the path ahead. Of course, she knows they are watching; Zoe and the C-Cups, right in her line of vision, watching her every step. She couldn't avoid them completely, she knows that. They wouldn't allow such a thing. *Just don't acknowledge them*, she thinks, grabbing her purse and coat. *Don't engage.*

Wait . . . something is missing. Her phone. It was right there on the small table by the rack. The HR Walk of Shame had happened so quickly, there'd been no time to grab her stuff, but she knew that's where she had left it. She can even see herself putting it there this morning, right before the chaos kicked in.

She walks back into the reception and scans it quickly.

"Olivia?" chirps a voice. "Are you okay?"

Ignore her, Olivia tells herself. *Where is it?*

"Are you looking for something?"

Fuck.

She turns slowly, eyes narrowed. There is Zoe, fresh as ever. Poreless and chipper, glossy lips pursed in faux-concern, and floaty white scarf tossed around her neck with strategic carelessness, à la Amelia Earhart.

It would be so easy, Olivia thinks. *To strangle her.*

"Where is it, Zoe?"

"Where's what?"

What do you think, bitch? "My phone, Zoe."

"Oh yes," Zoe says. "That."

To her left and right, the C-Cups giggle.

"You shouldn't leave it out like that. But don't worry, it's safe."

"Where?" says Olivia. Zoe pauses for a moment, then opens her mouth. It isn't a long pause, even—a few seconds, max—but long enough.

Long enough for Olivia to acknowledge that she has just been humiliated, demeaned and fired from her job. Long enough for her to acknowledge there are many people to question—Uni-Carol from HR, who hired her, and Marcus for being a ruthless, power-hungry corporate robot. Felix, for putting her in a game she was destined to lose. But the real villain? The true instigator of her downfall? This little nothing whose superficial pretty shell hides a dark and evil heart.

Just a few seconds before, Zoe opens her mouth to speak. Only instead of words, she's shrieking instead. Squealing, eyes darting around, looking for a place to hide as Olivia comes barreling towards her, teeth clenched, ready to rip her to shreds.

"Who the fuck do you think you are?" booms Olivia, and Zoe looks to her left and right, desperate for help. But the C-Cups are long gone, having already scattered to opposite sides of the room. "Come on Zoe, this is what you wanted, right? Let's finally have it out."

"What's wrong with you?" she squeaks, backing up. "You really are insane!"

"You have no idea," says Olivia. "I have allowed you to make me insane. This Salon is bullshit and full of nothing but atrocious, lying and total backstabbing fucking bitches! I don't have much to call mine anymore other than my daughter and mother, but I'll be damned if I lose my own integrity and sense of self to a bunch of pathetic and cruel subterranean scavengers. Especially you, Zoe. You are miserably inadequate and a pathetic excuse of a human being. You will get yours one day, too. Nasty bitch that you are. You should be working in the trash room. You lousy sack of shit."

"Why are you . . . wait, Olivia!" she squeaks. "I just wanted to tell you . . . I was just trying to . . ." Olivia cannot believe her ears and eyes. "You weren't trying to do anything." Announces Olivia. "Admit it, Zoe. All you wanted to do was get rid of me." Olivia feels liberated, relieved. Finally, and truly happy in this place. Happier than a 2.55 could ever make her.

Now they are just inches apart, their faces so close Olivia swears she can feel Zoe's breath on her cheeks. So close she can even make out—yes, there it is—one solitary infected pimple, flaring red and caked in foundation. Olivia has the last laugh, as she holds her head high, and exits the Salon for the last time. Just before she exits the Salon doors, she turns. "Goodbye, Bitches of Fifth Avenue. Classless acts. Thank you for everything. May I never see any of you ever again." With that, Olivia focuses on closing the Salon door, and thus in turn, opening a new door on what's to come.

Chapter Six

One Month Later

"Olivia!" shouts Gladys. "Olivia, where are you?"

Upstairs in her bedroom Olivia rolls her eyes. Her mother knows exactly where she is. Up in her childhood bedroom, surrounded by garment bags and dresses, skirts and blazers. They dangle from every hangable surface—the door frame, desk knobs. She's even taken pictures off the wall to use the nails to hang tees and belts.

Right now, she has six looks, but they don't feel cohesive. At the initial brainstorming session, the women had been all over the place. *I need something for the beach*, Ida Gottsagen had demanded. *Stewie and I are going on a cruise to Aruba! Royal Caribbean was having a special for repeat clients. We just couldn't say no! And we got a courtesy cabin upgrade!*

This isn't about your personal needs, said Lillian Sandran. *This is for a show!* She had ideas of her own, vying for a more sophisticated route. *Furs! They are sophisticated, timeless . . .*

Let's just hope PETA doesn't show, Joan Adler had muttered.

PETA? Said Lillian. *Please. They don't come to New Jersey.*

So, we've narrowed it down to bikinis and fox coats, Olivia had said. *That will make a statement.* The women had laughed, ultimately deferring to Olivia. In the end, she'd settled on spring looks. Fresh starts, women in bloom. *New beginnings, how does that sound?*

The women had loved it, and so did Olivia.

If anyone believed in new beginnings, it was her.

And now, surrounded by luxurious floral prints and chic pastels, age-appropriate pieces with flair, Olivia is starting to focus in on a cohesive vision. Good thing, too, with only a week until the annual Hadassah fundraiser . . . and their first fashion show.

Okay, so it wasn't CHANEL on a Parisian runway, but it was a place to start. She only had three days until the big event, and there was a lot to do. Final selections, fittings, checking in with the public relations director, an old childhood friend offering some PR support. *Oh, Olivia! How exciting. Of course, I will help for free. I could use some pro bono work for my portfolio.* Oh, and the lighting! She'd found Antoine, a great guy from the community theater circuit to help produce. He had real vision, she believed. He'd just spent the past four years working on an amateur Fiddler on the Roof production.

She picks up a Calvin Klein pencil dress, the daffodil yellow burst of spring sunshine—perfect for Libby Rottenberg, who was always upbeat, giddily excited over the smallest things. *Form-fitting, but it will work perfectly*, Olivia thinks. *For seventy-eight, Libby still had a rockin' bod.*

"Olllllivvvvvia!!!!!"

The sound is closer, at the bottom of the stairs. Olivia rolls her eyes. As always, her mother will not be ignored. No need to respond, she already hears the footsteps coming towards her.

"Darling, didn't you hear me?" Gladys stands at the door, slightly out of breath. "Ooooh! I love that dress. Is it for me?"

"Libby."

"Figures. That skinny-winny, I just hate her. But she'll look gorgeous! What a silhouette. The ruching is phenomenal, don't you think?"

Olivia can't help but smile. The women have really invested themselves in this show; they have scoured the local area, convincing high-end boutiques to offer loaner pieces, even getting them to donate money in the process. From the runway layout to the music, they've appointed themselves honorary fashion world experts, poring over magazines and discussing various lines with a Tim Gunn and Heidi Klum level of fashion confidence. Newfound devotees to Project Runway, Lena Weiss has even teased to potentially trying out. *So, my sewing skills are less than meh, but what does that matter? An adorable senior citizen, how could they say no?*

"You're right, Mom," says Olivia, smiling. "The ruching is great. But listen, I'm really busy."

"Yes, yes, I know, darling. But this is important. This is . . . *surprising*." She takes a dramatic pause, and Olivia internally sighs. Her Mom should have been an actress—whether discovering the milk has gone bad or finding an uber deal at Neiman Marcus's Last Call, she can make an Oscar-worthy dramatic moment out of anything.

"Yes? C'mon, Mom. Out with it."

"You have a visitor."

Olivia stares at her, surprised. She never gets . . . visitors.

"And he says he knows you from . . . Harper James."

What? Olivia feels the blood rush to her head. *Who could possibly . . . ?*

"What's his name?"

"Oh no, what was it?" says Gladys, genuinely distressed. "Oh shoot, I don't remember. But he seems very nice, Olivia. Very . . ." Eyes gleaming, she mouths one word with a witty grin: *handsome!*

After everything, Olivia is finally in a better place, with direction and serious goals. When she envisions the future, it isn't murky and dark—not clear, exactly, but brighter and with unknown promise. It hasn't been easy getting here, though. That's for sure.

Only now, the more recent past has returned. Directly entering her mother's very own house.

***

Those first few days after being let go from Harper James, she was in a state of shock. She ran through the events of that final day again and again, seeing it play out like scenes from a movie in her head. That boardroom meeting with those embarrassing film clips of her projected on that huge screen. The horror and confusion—the fury. Her entire life had been taken out of context and all her hard work dismissed. And nobody would listen or try to understand.

Then there was Zoe, that pretty and evil little troll.

Beneath her moisturized, microdermabrasioned, Botoxed, chemically-peeled, cosmetically-plastered glossy surface, Zoe was just a little girl. An almost child who'd never struggled and didn't know shit about the world.

One day you'll know what it feels like to suffer, Olivia had thought. *One day you'll know how it is to be down low in the fucking dirt. Then you'll have a choice to make yourself—just give yourself over to the pain or pick yourself up and keep moving forward.*

Or maybe she wouldn't. Maybe everything would stay the same, her life easy and charmed. She'd continue to manipulate and sabotage, surround herself with fearful acolytes, bully her way through life. Maybe Zoe was destined for success—but no matter how big her circle, no matter the plethora of kiss asses and faux-friends and desperate suck-ups, she'd still be alone. Maybe she would even marry one day, landing a rich, powerful man like Marcus—but chances are, beneath the surface, he'd be just as empty as she was.

You can have everything and still be alone. Olivia finally understood that. She had been, but she wasn't anymore.

Sure, those first few days she'd moped around, yet again in ripped tees and sweats, still in a state of confusion and shock. There were so many things she didn't understand. Why had she been the one they attacked like that? Felix being fired, Marcus taking over . . . that was upsetting, but not completely a surprise. But still, she didn't understand why she had been targeted, and so viciously. And where had they gotten that security footage?

She knew she could reach out to Felix and Marguerite. Both had called and sent texts. But she couldn't bring herself to respond, not yet. She'd done her best, she knew that, but she couldn't help what she felt . . . she let them down. *Gosh I also haven't spoken with Daphne in forever*, she thought. *I still need to call her and tell her about all of this bullshit.*

Three days after being fired, she got an email from HR. It was straight to the point: *this is to notify you of your official termination from the Harper James corporation.* A form letter, full of emotionless jargon. There has only been one moment of personalization.

In regard to the former employees' participation in a journalistic piece for the Women's Style Daily periodical, the magazine has been informed of all references, quotes and mentions of one Olivia Kopelman are to be removed from the piece, as she is no longer an associate/has no affiliation with the Harper James Salon. In addition, Olivia Kopelman is prohibited from communicating with anyone involved in such an article, including and not limited to the journalist, his associates at WSD and former Harper James Salon clients who participated in any capacity.

Blake, obviously, did not get this memo. He'd started reaching out the day after she was fired, his texts and voicemails growing more insistent. *What's going on, Olivia? I got a call from Harper James that made no sense. They said you no longer worked there. I'm confused.* In another, he'd told her they wanted her out of the article. *But they won't give me a reason, which is insane. No one will even tell me where you went.* The texts were even more to the point: *Where are you, Olivia? And please call me.* The last had simply been her name, followed by a question mark. *Olivia?*

As soon as she got the email from HR, she blocked his number. She hated doing it, but knew it was for the best. If they spoke, she'd say too much, she was sure of that. She'd jeopardize his vision, screw his perspective . . . get him in trouble, even. She might hate the Salon, but she liked him—no need to take him down with her. All her hard work had been in vain, and she didn't want to do that to him. Besides, he didn't need her, not really. Finding a replacement for his article would be no problem.

No doubt, Zoe had already stepped up to the plate.

As for blocking Marguerite and Felix, she'd felt even guiltier about that. But it wasn't forever, that's what she told herself. Their queries were just too painful to read; just listening to their voicemails, too much. It was only for now . . . just until she has moved on, gotten back on her feet. Just until it no longer hurt to see their names pop up on her cell phone screen.

True, those early days had been difficult, riddled with a sense of hopelessness and sad pipe dreams. But unlike the first time, when she'd left D.C. in a dark cloud, Olivia refused to let herself plummet into desperation.

Almost immediately, Olivia refused to give in to the pity, forcing herself to get up every morning and get dressed. Unlike last time, she vowed not to mope around the house in stained and ripped ragged tops and sweats—she would force herself to look presentable, even with nowhere to go.

Of course, Gladys could think of a few places.

In the beginning, Gladys and Gwynnie went to great lengths to comfort Olivia. It wasn't her fault, they insisted, Gladys even suggesting they seek an employment lawyer for a potential wrongful termination case. Olivia rejected the offer—the firing had been wrong, for sure, but she wasn't sure about the legal front. Either way, what would be the point of pursuing her firing legally? At best, there would be a settlement, but even if she could afford a lawyer, the last thing she wanted was to dredge up all the crap she'd just experienced. She just needed to put this behind her and move on. She needed to continue living, whatever that meant.

So, a week after her dramatic Harper James exit, when Gladys had insisted that they go shopping with her friend Shirley, Olivia had simply shrugged. "Why not?" she'd said. "I've got nothing else to do."

It had been fun, and Olivia had fallen right back into her old ways, helping Shirley pick pieces for an upcoming dinner and Temple mixer. She'd oohed and ahhhed over Olivia's selections, marveling at her taste. "I'd never think of trying a skirt that length, but it's perfect! This one has remarkable fashion sense, Gladys." After she'd rung up her purchases, Shirley had grabbed Olivia's hand. "I can't thank you enough, wonderful girl. So, where do I send the check?" Olivia had been too stunned to speak, which was fine—Gladys stepped right in, calculating Olivia's commission and informing Shirley she could simply Venmo the fee.

"I can't believe you, Mom," Olivia said once Shirley had departed. "That was so sneaky! I was just giving her fashion advice."

"You're an expert, Olivia. Your advice is worth something. Besides, she practically begged me."

"I see. And it wasn't your suggestion, I suppose? You didn't, maybe, plant the idea in her head?"

"Sarcasm doesn't suit you dear. And, of course, I did. But it didn't take much, I'll tell you that. Shirley knows you were at Harper James, and she knows you have style in your blood. So maybe I made a little suggestion, but she jumped right on board. I mean, how often does the old lady crowd have access to a trained, expert stylist around here?"

Olivia had just shaken her head and smiled. "I love you, Mom."

"As you should. And you'll love me even more after she tells her friends."

Gladys had been right. By the next week, word had spread amongst Shirley's crowd, and Olivia had already scheduled several clients—seems her services were quite marketable amongst the retired Jersey Hadassah Northeast Chapter 18 set. So much so that the organization's President, Ida Gottsagen, had a revelation: for that year's big fundraiser, *Olivia should put together a fashion show! It'll be wonderful,* Ida explained, y*ou'll help raise money and advertise your personal styling business!* Olivia hadn't realized she'd unknowingly started a personal styling business, but who was she to argue? Besides, it made her feel useful again, like she had a purpose. Despite all that had happened, she still loved fashion, and loved helping women feel beautiful.

She'd even made a call that was long overdue. Daphne.

"Hi," Olivia had started, not believing Daphne had actually answered on the first ring. "I know this is sudden, but it's me, Olivia."

"Olivia!" She'd squealed. "Where have you been? I almost hired a private investigator! Goodness, I've been worried. Now, my darling, what is going on with you?!"

"I'm so sorry, Daphne. You simply cannot believe the quicksand shit show I've been caught in."

"I'm happy to hear your voice, darling."

"Then why are you crying?" asked Olivia.

"I've missed you!"

It had been a long conversation—several hours—as Olivia had apologized again and again for disappearing, Daphne insisting it was fine and that she understood. "You're back, that's what matters. Now tell me everything!"

Olivia had done as she was told, filling her old friend in on all that had happened . . . it was a lot. Daphne had listened to every word carefully, reliving the Harper James Salon events bit by bit with Olivia, going from surprise to shock to rage and back again. "Horrible," she kept saying. "Utterly disturbing! They did what? This Zoe . . . how dare she? Abhorrent, Olivia. She's a disgrace!"

At the end, hearing of Olivia's new endeavors, her feelings had changed completely. "Wonderful!" she'd gushed. "Good! Exactly right! You need to be out on your own, as I always said. With a talent like yours . . . you need to call the shots. The cream always rises to the top, Olivia. Never forget that."

They'd made plans to see each other soon, Daphne suggesting she come to DC. "I have so many women who'd like to hire you," she said. We'll expand your business to Washington. Lord knows these women could use you here."

"I couldn't," Olivia had said, shocked. "There's no way they'd want to see me, not with my reputation."

"Phooey, Olivia. Do you think anyone cares? The world moves on. I mean, have you watched the news? This town is in chaos, every day a fresh hell. I myself know three people who have been called in by the Attorney General, and several who very well may be indicted. There's even talk of impeachment. And Edwin . . . he's yesterday's news. And his former wife? Talented, beautiful and ready to take over the world. Trust me on this, darling. You are your own brand . . . and now you're making your own stunning and fabulous life!"

***

Between appointments and preparations for the show, the days that followed had been packed. And the busier she was, the less she thought about what had happened, or how things had ended. Of course, it was still there, and would surface at unexpected moments—*How dare Marcus screw me like that?* She'd wonder suddenly, while Gwynnie was describing her latest social cause. Or when buying cereal at the market, she'd think *I wonder what Zoe is doing right now?* In those moments, the anger would rise, washing over her.

Just as quickly, she would push those thoughts out of her head. Pay for her purchase, ask Gwynnie to tell her more, think about what she could do to make life better *here and now*. As each day passed, and her to do list increased, thoughts of Harper James became less and less.

***

Some experiences stay with you, Olivia realizes. No matter how hard you try to push them away, they will surface again.

In this case, right at your front door.

"Are you sure he's with Harper James?" asks Olivia. At the doorway, her mother nods.

"I see," says Olivia, glancing at her reflection. She pats down her hair, straightens her crew neck top. She looks good, at least. She's started getting regular sleep. One benefit of being embarrassingly let go from her Salon job. It's done wonders for her skin. "Well, I suppose I should go downstairs," says Olivia. "See exactly who this person might be."

"No need, darling," says Gladys, a guilty look crossing her face. "I knew you were busy, so I brought him up," she says, motioning to someone. "He's right at the end of the hall."

Before Olivia has time to say *WTF, you did what?* Or even fully process this information, her mother has ducked out of sight. "Right in here! Come on in," she says, stepping back into the room. "What did you say your name was again?"

The man appears, wearing 501 jeans and a sheepish grin.

"Blake," he tells her, though his eyes are focused on someone else.

A long pause.

"Well, I'll leave you to it," says Gladys, ducking out the door.

After Gladys excuses herself, there is another long silence. "So," Blake finally says. "Miss me?"

"How did you find me?"

"Googled Gladys Kopelman."

"Who told you my mother's name?"

"I found it . . . soon after we met. I'm a journalist, Olivia."

"So, you knew about . . . my past. Edwin, D.C. You knew everything."

"Yeah. I didn't think it was appropriate to mention."

"But it was appropriate to come here?" Having him show up here was strange enough, but the fact he knew about her is even more disconcerting. Olivia feels unnerved, raw.

"No, it wasn't appropriate. Not at all. I just . . . well, I'm here now." He stands there uncomfortably, looking down at the floor with a nervous smile. "Hey, maybe I could sit down for a minute?"

"You won't be staying long. So that stuff about my being mysterious, that was all, what? Bullshit?"

"Not at all. You were mysterious. You are." He shakes his head. "Look, I tried to get you to tell me about yourself . . . I nudged. But you didn't want to, and I get that. We all have pasts, right? Me, for instance. You know I used to be a political reporter, right?"

Olivia nods.

"You read some of my stuff?"

"What I could find. It was from a while back."

"Because I haven't done that kind of reporting in years. Want to know why?"

"Not really. I don't think that I care. I really don't think I want you here."

"I fucked everything up," he says, ignoring her. "Look, I came all the way here. May I at least sit down?"

"Fine," says Olivia, moving a stack of clothes from the desk chair. "But listen, Blake . . . I'm sure you had the best intentions . . . and none of this is your fault. I should have returned your calls, so that's on me. But . . . I'm trying to move on with my life, okay? There's nothing to discuss."

"This isn't about you, it's about me," he says, sitting. "So yeah, I was a political reporter, and really good at it. Just out of grad school and confident. Way too confident, really. Fancied myself some sort of Hunter S. Thompson in the making."

Olivia sits on the bed with a sigh.

"Got a great job at a big media conglomerate and proved myself right away. I'd do anything for a story." Stake out the condo of a congressman all night just for a quote, go through their trash for notes they'd thrown away . . . embarrassing to think of now. I wanted to unmask corruption, make the world a better place. Even if I had to get in the dirt to do it. But it worked, you see. Remember Evers Everett?"

"The Senator? Yeah, that guy was awful," says Olivia, remembering. A one-time bastion of conservative values, Evers had embraced the right wing. Advocating for Jesus, the sanctity of marriage and a return to morality . . . until the surfacing of covert bribes, mistresses and embezzling from non-profits. The headlines were everywhere.

"That story broke two years ago. Only I had it long before that."

"You did?"

"Yeah. Had the sources, the evidence. The article was ready to go, and I was on top of the world, feeling like a total badass. I was going to get a Pulitzer, I figured. I was going to cement myself in journalism history." He laughs. "What a cocky egomaniac. Still, it was a big deal."

"What happened?"

"The higher-ups nixed it. Seems the CEO and Evers were golf buddies. You probably wouldn't know his name, but he's a big deal. A Rupert Murdoch type, though he prefers a lower profile. So, I demanded to see him, got in for a meeting and . . . threw a fit. Said blocking the story was unethical, reprehensible . . . said he had a responsibility to report the truth. Told him if he wouldn't print it, someone else would." He laughs, remembering. "I was wrong there. Within 24 hours, not only was I jobless, but no one in the journalism world would take my calls. Within a month, I was broke, had an eviction notice and couldn't get a gig at *Cat Weekly*. So, I ran and hid at my mom's retirement home in South Beach. Kinda like you're doing now."

"And the story came out anyway."

"Yup, but not for years. I spent that time doing everything else but journalism. Substitute teaching, customer service for a phone line. Finally got enough nerve to move back to New York and get my own place. By own place, I mean a closet in an illegal warehouse I shared with sixteen other guys. But things got better. Ran into an old friend from Columbia . . . okay, waited on an old friend from Columbia. I was serving at this high-priced Italian restaurant."

"Seriously, I get that you're trying to offer some sort of lesson here," says Olivia. "Some insight. But it won't change anything, so you really didn't have to come all this way."

"So," says Blake, ignoring her. "He'd ended up in the fashion journalism world and took pity on me. *Can I help?* He asked. No one in the political world will touch me, that's what I told him. He said, *that was a long time ago, man. They just might. But you need a job now and guess what industry cares less about your sordid past in the political world?* I told him I didn't know anything about fashion, and he just laughed. *No one really does*, he says. *They make it up as they go along."*

"Wow," says Olivia. The story is so enthralling, she's forgotten how weird it is, him being there. "And so, you wrote your first piece?"

"I did. I just approached it the way I had politics. Look for the truth beneath the hype, the real story beyond the spin. Unmask what is really going on behind the scenes, both good and bad. Turns out, I was good at it. *Am* good at it. That's what I've been doing for the past several years, covering the fashion world. Only this time, with a lot less ego and minus the TMZ tactics." He smiles. "At least, most of the time."

Olivia nods. "You *are* good at it, Blake. You see fashion in a fresh way and don't hold back."

"Losing everything opens your eyes. Frees you up to take risks. You know that as well as I do."

Olivia gives him a sad and pathetic smile. "Look, I'm sorry I was so rude. It was nice of you to come here. And telling me that story . . . I mean, I get it, I do. But I'm going to be okay. I haven't given up, not even on fashion. I mean, just look at this room."

"Wait, Olivia . . . you misunderstood. My point was that . . ."

"Your point was that you feel bad. You know that article incited jealousy, and that jealousy was partially to blame for my getting fired. But it was only one part, Blake. And it was nice of you to come, you're a good guy. But I'm not your responsibility."

"That's not why I'm here." He shakes his head, smiling. "Look, Olivia, you've got this all wrong. I'm not here to give you a pep talk . . . you don't need it. You're one of the . . . strongest women I've ever met. Most talented, too. You'll be fine no matter what, I know that. I knew that when they told me you'd been fired. The thing that I didn't know? *Why* you'd been fired."

"The reason is not important."

"That's the last thing you tell a journalist."

"But you finished the article, right?"

"I did. And that's another reason. I figured you wouldn't read it, so I came here to make sure you did."

"Why would I want to? The last thing I want to read about is Harper James. Especially that damn Salon."

"They probably wish everyone felt that way," he says with a cryptic smile. "It came out this morning, that's why I'm here so early. Wanted to see your face when you read it. The print edition sold out almost immediately. The web version exploded."

"Web version?"

"Yes, with the full visuals." He reaches into his messenger bag and pulls out a laptop. Flips it open, hits a few buttons. "So, you see, I had no choice. I had to come here and watch you read every word."

He turns the computer around, stopping her cold. *Out of Fashion*, reads the headline. *The Harper James Salon and Fall of an Iconic Retailer.*

"Give me that thing," says Olivia. "Now."

***

Sitting on her bed, heart pounding and eyes fixed to the screen, Olivia reads. The article begins simply enough.

"By the late 1940's, America was still living in post-WWII purgatory. The war had come to an end many years earlier, yet the repercussions remained apparent, permeating every aspect of daily life. You could even see it in the attire—many women still dressed in the uniform of wartime, their attire a drab utilitarian minimalism dictated by ration cards and patriotism.

Yet, come 1947, a dramatic shift—a new visionary burst onto the scene. Christian Dior's aesthetic was far from sensible, thrifty asexuality—hyper feminine, he'd traded the drab war-era austereness for bright bursts of colors, decadent textures and generous amounts of fabric. The connotations were obvious: gone were the days of belt-tightening and worry; this was the new era of glamor."

Nothing controversial or eye-opening, at least not yet. Maybe it was a tease, the headline, ultimately amounting to very little real critique.

Olivia isn't sure whether to be disappointed or relieved.

The writing is good, though, she must admit that. *Maybe . . . could that be the real reason he is here?* She wonders. *For an ego boost?*

She feels Blake from across the room, watching her read, eyes fixed on her face. *I won't look up*, she thinks. *I won't give him the satisfaction.*

Back to the computer screen.

"With the establishment of their flagship 5th Avenue store, Harper James would represent that transition, cementing its reputation as one of the guiding forces in high-end fashion. This legacy has proven enduring—even today, the name Harper James is synonymous with classic, ladylike elegance.

Ladylike, thinks Olivia. *That's a laugh.*

"Amongst the many departments at Harper James—now a franchise with half a dozen stores worldwide—the 5th Avenue Flagship remains their most prized institution. And of their many departments there, one stands above all others. A mecca for the most discerning, elite of clientele, the Harper James Salon, their exclusive personal styling department, has gained the most enduring legacy. Frequented by legends that range from Jackie Onassis and Princess Di to modern A-listers and socialites, the Salon has been seen as the embodiment of everything Harper James represents, elegance, exclusivity, unparalleled customer service and impeccable taste.

You forgot catty bitches, client stealing and backstabbing manipulation, thinks Olivia. *What is this, propaganda?* She sighs, feeling her annoyance rise.

"Last month, I was contacted by Harper James management with a rare opportunity—I was to be granted unprecedented access to the legendary personal shopping Salon for an extended amount of time. As a journalist, my job is to chronicle a story from a distance. Yet, in the fifty plus hours I spent there, I became an unintentional participant in what can only be called a locale in upheaval. The Salon is a microcosm for the state of the fashion industry in general, I came to understand, perfectly exemplifying the clash of old and new, the golden age of glamor and how it is changing, both in negative and positive ways, in our fast-paced, digital world. In my time at the Salon, I witnessed the unfiltered inner workings, watched several client fittings, conducted extensive interviews and came to know this highly discreet, iconic department in a way few ever have. And in doing so, I have reached a well-informed yet unfortunate conclusion: past reputation may be just that, and a glamorous facade might as well hide cracks just beneath the surface.

For decades, Harper James has been lauded as the pinnacle of taste from the highest rungs of leadership down—a home to those with sublime fashion expertise, old-fashioned good manners and impeccable style. Come to find out, this reputation is outdated, and the old guard has been replaced. And from my personal observations, this new guard is best summed up as a fad-driven, youth obsessed, corporate import whose sole objective is to up sales numbers and constantly pad the bottom line.

Oh my God, thinks Olivia. *Did he just . . .*

"This attitude isn't limited to the board room, either—in the time I spent at the Salon, in their iconic personal shopping department, I saw this culture of dismissive mediocrity permeate every aspect of the establishment, from the top floor of the legendary 5th Avenue establishment down to the first-floor cosmetics haven.

He did. Pulse racing, Olivia leans in close, reading faster.

"While I saw little attempt to honor the Harper James legacy or fashion artistry, I was privy to Salon employee misconduct in various other arenas. And as my assigned hostess became a pawn in these games, without realizing it, I did as well. From the first moment, Olivia Kopelman struck me as the ideal Salon employee . . ."

Oh my God. Olivia's head snaps up. "I can't believe you! My name? How could you possibly think that was ok?"

"Just keep reading, Olivia," says Blake, jumping to his feet. "Please. Just finish, and then I swear, you can scream at me all you want, okay? You can scream and hit me and . . ."

"Just shut up," she spit out. "Shut up and let me finish."

Olivia speed reads the next part, all about her. He's flattering towards her, speaking of her talent, her gift with clients. He gives her background, but revealing nothing too personal, speaking of how she worked her way up the Harper James ladder. How she was brought into the Salon based on talent, and despite her "non-traditional training for such a position"—*if by non-traditional you mean non-existent*, thinks Olivia, almost laughing—yet explaining that once she was installed in the position, Olivia immediately shone.

"A lesson in bringing classic Harper James values to the modern era, Olivia merged fashion expertise with customer service and respect for retail legacy with an openness to the modern woman's unique challenges and needs. Sophisticated, beautiful, authentic and good at her job, I knew right away—Olivia Kopelman wouldn't last.

Beautiful, thinks Olivia. *Sophisticated . . . does he really think that?* Olivia feels herself blush. *Don't look up*, she tells herself. *Keep reading.*

"Olivia's fate had been predetermined, just like all the others. From my first day in the Salon, I knew how the other employees saw her—as a threat."

Olivia reads the next part, fast, hardly believing the words. He introduces several of the girls, focusing specifically on a spiteful, minimally talented mid twenty-something hell-bent on ruling the Salon by any means possible. Unlike Olivia, he doesn't use her real name, informing the reader he's chosen a pseudonym to protect the women still working in the Salon.

Not for long, thinks Olivia. *If people believe what they're reading.*

"Born into privilege and achieving the job via highly placed family connections, according to a high-level Harper James source, "Allie" had a modicum level of talent but little respect for values intrinsic to the Salon of yesteryear. But what she does have, by this reporters' own observations, is a hunger for power, and the willingness to squash anyone who might jeopardize that goal by outshining her. In other words, a woman like Olivia Kopelman."

Olivia scans the next section as though in a dream—it's right there, all of it. A quick rundown of various infractions and manipulations, demeaning behavior and calculated sabotage, perpetrated by one woman. A woman whose real name might be slightly different, but whose real-life actions have been laid out for the world to see, right there on the page, in black and white:

"Considering the depths to which 'Allie' was willing to sink, Olivia didn't stand a chance. She was destined to be pushed out, be cast aside, along with others who embraced the values Harper James was founded on—quality, craftsmanship and the best of high-end retail. In many cases, the very men and women who had, through decades of service, helped create that reputation. In fact, the very man who offered me this exclusive, Felix Dupont—a thirty-year veteran of the establishment whose eye for style and refined taste are retail industry legend—has since left of his own accord."

"Wait . . . Felix didn't quit . . . he was fired!"

Blake nods his head. "The information is correct . . . who do you think was my best source? He would have been fired soon enough, he just sped up the process. He stood up for what he believed in, even knowing the consequences. Then he quit before they could fire him."

"What could have been so important that he'd jeopardize his job?"

"The unwarranted firing of his most cherished protégé by a bullshit Advisory Board," said Blake. Then, softer . . . *pp* or *pianissimo* in musical terms. "You, Olivia. You were important enough."

"I can't . . . I don't . . . why didn't he tell me, Blake?"

"He tried, just like me. You wouldn't answer his calls. Marguerite either. She wanted to explain why Willard left . . ."

"Wait. He wasn't fired either?"

"No, his son was."

"Devon? I don't understand."

"It wasn't about his capability. It was about what he wasn't capable of doing."

"I don't understand."

"Marcus made a request, and Devon refused. Told him it was inappropriate, unethical. Maybe even legally questionable. Something that big had to go through proper channels, that's what he said. When Marcus insisted, saying he was in charge, Devon still refused. *You've only been COO for two days, and either way, it's not happening.*"

"What request?"

"Security footage. Devon wouldn't hand it over. But when he came in the next day, it was gone anyway. So, he backed up the remaining Salon footage on a server—not all of it, he didn't have time, but the last few months—then erased the drive. Then he wrote his resignation on the back of a Chinese takeout menu. It said, if I remember correctly, *I'm out of here, effective immediately. You guys suck.* Oh, and his name."

"How do you know all this?"

"He was a source. Willard too."

"Willard?"

"Soon as Devon quit, he put in his resignation as well."

"But his pension . . ."

"Don't worry about that. Devon was just there for his dad, but the kid will be fine, and so will his dad. He's already being headhunted by the security departments of a Fortune 500 company and Google. Oh, and the fact he invested in Bitcoin early on. Devon doesn't have to work at all, he just chooses to. Like his dad. Fact is, he wanted Willard to quit years ago. Said he'd take care of everything, but . . . his dad is stubborn. Luckily, because of all this, he changed his tune. Devon's already convinced him he needs a house . . . even scoping out one to buy him. Well, Marguerite might have had a part in the convincing, I gotta say. *Stop being a stubborn ass*, I think those were the words she used. *Let your son take care of you.* Like I said, I had plenty of sources . . . all members of the Olivia fan club."

This makes Olivia smile, despite the shock. Still, she is confused. "But they all left over some . . . footage? It doesn't make sense."

"Not just some footage, Olivia. Footage from one specific day. Footage that could be edited and presented out of context."

It takes a second before everything clicks into place. Could it be true? It's so ludicrous, so awful, Olivia can't help but laugh.

"Me. I was on that footage. All those clips they played when they fired me . . . they were filmed the same day."

"Exactly."

"But . . . wait. It was Marcus who made the demand of Devon, right? But why did he . . . I mean, how did Marcus . . . even know that footage existed?"

"How much have you read?" he asks, pointing to the computer screen.

"Just a few paragraphs left."

"Finish it. There's a surprise ending."

Olivia nods, eyes returning to the screen. And somehow, despite her reeling brain, she makes it through.

"The Harper James Salon may well be a microcosm for the changing face of high-end retail. Customer needs set aside for those of the employees themselves; a dedication to fashion less important than a dedication to personal self-interest. Instead of honing their craft, Salon employees like Allie have dedicated themselves to far less lofty pursuits—backstabbing, cattiness, strategic manipulation, and immoral behavior. All these behaviors, in keeping with the declining Harper James value system itself, are exercised with specific goals that have little to do with fashion—rising in the ranks, gaining power and increasing sales numbers.

While initially sent to cover the most exclusive department in the store, the private shopping experience that has come to be known simply as *The Salon*, I quickly discovered the hidden, dark underbelly of this high-stakes retail universe. If anything is indicative of Harper James's fall from grace, it is this once illustrious department. While reporting this story, I not only became a part of it, but was granted access to private footage which will allow the world to see as well. For the sake of privacy, the faces have been blurred and voices muted. Yet, the actions, all performed during business hours on Harper James property, speak volumes enough in themselves.

In the modern climate of mass-production, branding and demographics, retailers have a choice to make—evolve with grace, or simply throw it all away. After my time in the Salon, I've seen the second option firsthand, and it served as a warning.

Now you will too."

Olivia scrolls down. "Oh, my God . . . there are movies."

"Short video segments, yes. Footage."

"How did you . . . *oh*." She shakes her head, understanding. "Devon. The server."

"Exactly," says Blake, standing. He walks over, sits next to her on the bed. He's so close their thighs are touching. Olivia thinks, *hmmm interesting.*

Blake puts his hand on the mousepad. They look at each other and are so close she smells his personal fragrance, Creed's *Aventus*.

"Ready?" asks Blake.

Olivia has no idea, but she nods anyway. She watches, as it plays out like a movie script before her eyes . . .

A flash of light, an image. Video begins to play. The footage is not professional—grainy, black and white—yet clear enough to see details. A vast room, shot from above. Polished wood floors, high ceilings. This is THE SALON.

Designer Deceit

An average workday woman walking back and forth. An elegant TALL WOMAN slinks through the frame. Another employee—GIRL ONE—crosses her path. They do not acknowledge each other. GIRL ONE is wearing a short skirt and carries a large fountain drink in her hand. She sips as she walks; she moves remarkably fast in six-inch heels.

CUT TO:

Another camera, simultaneous. Another employee—GIRL TWO—stands next to a platform. Posed on top, a CLIENT; she is heavy-set, yet clad in a dress several sizes too small. She contemplates her reflection in a tri fold mirror; based on her body language, she does not feel confident. Below her, GIRL ONE, wearing a frilly dress, offers critique; based on her body language, the comments are affirmations meant to satiate the uncomfortable client. At the same time as offering commentary, GIRL ONE also covertly stifles a giggle. She notices something offscreen—someone. Unbeknownst to CLIENT, she beckons that person . . . .

Seconds later, GIRL ONE pops into the shot, still sipping her drink. Even with the blurred faces, the resemblance between GIRL ONE and GIRL TWO is obvious—they could be sisters, even twins. GIRL TWO nods to the platform; GIRL ONE follows the nod. Upon seeing the fat woman in a too tight dress, both GIRLS erupt into silent, yet near hysterical, hilarity.

Just out of eyeshot from the platform, with CLIENT completely unaware for the next sixty seconds, GIRL ONE and GIRL TWO perform silent mockery of heavyset CLIENT using various techniques—GIRL ONE puffs out her cheeks; GIRL TWO waddles in a circle, performing a crude imitation. Both point out various parts of the heavyset woman's body with a mixture of humorous mockery and disdain; they make pig faces and laugh silently.

CLIENT, still on the platform, remains unaware; she is lost in the dissatisfaction of her own image staring back at her. Suddenly, she unexpectedly turns; GIRL ONE is faster. By the time CLIENT spots GIRL ONE and GIRL TWO, they have regained their composure. Now GIRL TWO joins GIRL ONE in conversing with CLIENT; based on their body language, they are offering gushing praise of her current attire.

CUT TO:

The same locale, another day. GIRL ONE and GIRL TWO are wearing different clothes, although GIRL ONE still maintains a short hemline and ultra-high heels. The dressing area has been blocked off for privacy's sake, hidden from the main Salon by several dividers. Behind the barrier, the space is different than in previous footage; the platform is barely visible, now jumbled with discarded accessories and shoes; designer clothes have been haphazardly strewn across the remaining areas. Couture has been thrown over mirrors, the backs of chairs or simply left in crumpled piles on the floor.

Amidst the disarray, a YOUNG CLIENT sits on the floor. She is wearing a half-zipped designer dress pulled up to her thighs. Between her knees, an enormous bottle of champagne. To her left and right, GIRL ONE and GIRL TWO. All are laughing hysterically while periodically passing the bottle and drinking. GIRL TWO suddenly rises to her feet—a slight stumble as she gains her footing. She quickly scurries to a table in the corner, then leans down and snorts. YOUNG CLIENT watches the action; based on her body language, she is annoyed. Words are exchanged, and GIRL TWO rejoins the others, this time walking with slow care. In her hand, a small cosmetic mirror with several white lines.

"That's a famous young socialite," says Blake, pointing to the girl on the screen. Her name is . . ."

"Amber Timberly."

"Exactly. She was identified on Tik Tok, even with the blurred face. So were her personal shoppers, Chrissy and Catie."

"Oh wow . . ."

"Keep watching. This next part is really something."

CUT TO:

The breakroom. A woman slinks in, making an effort not to be seen. It is the TALL WOMAN employee from the earlier scene. Moving quickly, she opens the fridge and removes a plate of muffins. Quick as lightning, she licks the top of each, then replaces the plate in the fridge. She moves to close the fridge door, then stops suddenly, reaching for a large plastic cup with a straw on top. She removes the lid, spits in the drink, reattaches the lid and returns the drink to the fridge. She exited the breakroom as quickly as she arrived.

"Seriously?" blurts Olivia, shocked. "Gia? She has it together . . . she's so polished, so refined."

"That place is so toxic, everyone feels it," says Blake. "Guess she was channeling aggression. She just found a unique way."

"A gross way. Good thing I always went out to lunch."

CUT TO:

Main room camera. An OLDER EMPLOYEE dressed in layers of fabric rushes through the salon with a rolling rack; it comes loose, tripping her. She stumbles, tries to catch herself on the rack; she falls anyway, crashing head first onto the floor. The rolling rack drags her half a foot before coming to a halt. Next to her, a STERN-LOOKING EMPLOYEE in combat boots has seen the whole thing; she makes no effort to help, but simply stands there, hands on hips, shaking her head. She stares at OLDER EMPLOYEE sprawled beneath her and walks on.

"These are horrible," says Olivia. "How many are there?"

"Just a few more," Blake tells her. "But watch these next ones carefully . . . there's a theme."

CUT TO:

Same angle. GIRL ONE heading out for the evening; she's wearing her jacket and has an enormous purse slung over her shoulder. GIRL ONE stops nonchalantly, noticing a dress on a rack that has been left behind. She touches the fabric, as though curious about the texture. A second later, the rack is empty, the dress having been covertly shoved in her purse. GIRL ONE continues towards the Salon exit as though nothing has happened.
CUT TO:

GIRL TWO pulling the same move, only with far more finesse. Much nervous darting of eyes as she reaches across a table, grabs a jeweled clutch and shoves it under her shirt. A quick turn: she races in the opposite direction so fast she nearly topples over in her skyscraper heels.

"No way . . . you have to be kidding me."

"Just wait," says Blake. "There are more."

CUT TO:

GIRL ONE swiping a designer shawl . . .

CUT TO:

GIRL TWO pocketing a pair of earrings from a table of designer accessories . . . .

CUT TO:

New angle. STERN-LOOKING EMPLOYEE from the previous scene, wearing the same combat boots. She stands at a shelf crammed with shoeboxes. She runs her hand down the line, stops at one and removes the box. Shoebox is opened, contents observed; STERN-LOOKING EMPLOYEE nonchalantly removes the new pair of buckled leather ankle boots, takes out the crumpled paper inside. Combat boots off, ankle boots on; paper stuffed in combat boots, and they are placed inside of the new shoebox. Lid is closed and the box is returned to the shelf.

"This is insane!" Says Olivia, pausing the video. "How did they get away with this stuff? I mean, why didn't anybody notice? Report it?"

"Maybe no one saw. And even if it was reported, there's a chance the higher ups would overlook it. Turns out, certain members of the Salon had closer ties to upper management than you might imagine. Close enough to make bad things go away."

"What does that mean?"

"Let me show you," says Blake, then reaches over and clicks play on the video. "This is actually the big finish."

Olivia turns to the screen, anxious of what awaits her. The footage ends with a montage; quick edits spliced together, but with a commonality.

CUT TO:

The breakroom—A MAN shot from behind, leaning against the counter, his face not visible. Below him, you can just make out the top of a head, a scarf tied around it, headband-style. The head, belonging to A WOMAN, moves back and forth, picking up speed; the man throws back his head in a moan.

CUT TO:

Main room. The Salon after hours. Lighting is dim, but you can just make out two figures at the center of the room. The same MAN, standing, legs splayed apart; behind him, a woman, much shorter. THE WOMAN from earlier, it can be assumed. She is taking something from around her neck—a scarf—and wrapping it around his wrists. Her actions are slow, methodical; once the fabric has been wrapped, she makes a knot. A sharp tug to the end, and she marches around to his front. Furiously unbuckles his pants, unzips him and violently pulls them down. His pants fall to his ankles, and he throws back his head and laughs. She steps forward, pulls back a hand, slaps him across the face. He freezes, going completely still. THE WOMAN steps back, gives a little nod . . . then drops to her knees.

CUT TO:

THE WOMAN reflected three ways in a tri fold mirror. The image is clearer—it is broad daylight, and she is kneeled just below a platform. THE MAN steps into the shot, this time his face in view . . .

The face is blurred, but their identities are obvious. That thick dark hair, the lanky, yet muscular body . . . Marcus. And the woman? That one is easy. And unlike the other ones, this is during the day, the footage bright.

Olivia knows the locale. Zoe's fitting room, with a platform to the right, just barely out of sight from the reception. The film has been strategically blurred, and not just on the faces in the film—but still, the actions are distinct and obvious.

Zoe. She knows the risk she is taking. This is during the day, she is only barely out of sight . . . at any moment, the C-Cups might rush in with gossip, or a coworker perhaps stopping by to take orders for a coffee run. But there she is, hard at work. Working fast, true—her movements are quick and precise, showing expertise—but taking a risk beyond belief.

And that man, with his shiny hair—even blurred, it is obvious his gaze is focused below. Even blurred, she knows that he wears a smirk; she knows the look on his face. That he's watching the girl below with satisfaction, an expression that says *I'm untouchable, I'm in control, I own everything I see.*

But wait . . . the scarf. That scarf Zoe is wearing, tied in a floppy bow on her head. Olivia remembers that scarf.

The day Marcus visited the Salon! She remembers it distinctly, how silly it looked. And this must be . . . the tour of her dressing room. That tour that seemed to last uncomfortably long. She watches Zoe at work, moving faster and faster, bow flopping more vigorously with each bob of her head . . .

We were right there. Just beyond that platform.

All the Salon employees, Olivia included, mere feet away. Wondering if they'd done well, impressed the visiting VIP. *Did they show themselves off? What did he think? Are we an asset, valuable employees? That's what we were thinking*, Olivia tells herself. *We were wondering if we made an impression . . . while right across the room, just barely hidden from view . . . Zoe is making one for sure.*

He didn't even unbuckle his pants. Just stands there while Zoe drops, unzips and then begins her task.

For some reason, this part bothers Olivia most of all.

Olivia sarcastically considers the scene; *Maybe he had limited time with the Salon employees—that's understandable, he's a busy professional. But if one goes so far as to blow you, well . . . the least you can do is open your own pants. I mean, it's the least he could do.*

"Olivia . . . Olivia, are you okay?"

"What?" says Olivia, snapping into reality. She looks down at the screen—the video is over. She saw it end with her own eyes. Yet, for some reason, it kept going in her head.

Shock. She's in shock.

"Seriously, Olivia . . . how do you feel? You don't look so great."

"I'm just . . . I don't know. That was a lot."

Blake nods.

"So that explains it, I guess," she says, the realization hitting her. "Why Marcus was out to get me. It wasn't personal, I guess. It had nothing to do with my quality of work, or the fact that I turned him down for a date . . . I mean, maybe that was my real mistake. If I'd just blown him like Zoe, I'd still have my job. I'd probably have a promotion, even."

"You don't mean that . . . wait. He asked you to blow him?"

Does Blake sound . . . jealous?

Olivia shakes her head. "Not in so many words. I didn't let him get that far. He's . . . repulsive. I wouldn't touch him to save my life. But he was never out to get me, not personally. I see that now. He was just doing what he was told. I mean, she tied him up, slapped him . . . he liked that kind of thing. How hard would it be for her to convince him?"

"You had to go? Well, it took her a while. He knew how good you were at your job, so it wasn't easy. You lasted a long time, so . . . so that's something."

"Yeah, I guess." Olivia gives a bitter laugh. "I should thank him for that."

"Listen, Olivia, I know this—"

"Is what? A shock? You're right. But it's also . . . I mean, it's almost impressive. I mean, Zoe is really good. Not just at blow jobs, even. Though shit, she obviously has talent there. Like, if they gave PhD's in sucking dick, well . . ."

"Olivia, it's okay . . ."

"No, Blake. I'm serious," she says, rising to her feet. "She convinced him to set me up, that's how good she is. She got me fired, that's just how remarkable her fucking goddamn blow job skills really are. She's so fucking talented; they should enact a golden honorary Academy award "Best in Blow" solely so they can present it to . . . Zoe! Best Actress in a leading role for Blow Jobs!"

"Olivia, stop!"

Something in his voice stops her cold. "She knows how to control men and get what she wants. It has nothing to do with sex, not really. A guy like Marcus, always in control . . . she slapped him around, tied him up, got him to do risky stuff. For once, he wasn't in control, and he liked that. Had it been some other guy . . . the kind who secretly longs to play the hero . . . well, she'd try another tactic. Talk in a baby voice, call him crying at 2:00 a.m. because she heard a scary noise. She doesn't have any magic power . . . she's a master manipulator."

"But why, then," says Olivia, disgusted by the hurt in her own voice. "Why target me of all people?"

"Because that's all she's got. She can manipulate and bully and sabotage, but she'll never have the one thing she wants. The thing you were born with . . . aptitude . . . flair . . . talent and charm. Whatever you want to call it. That's why I had to get this story out. Sure, it's important . . . a commentary on the state of the retail industry. But that's not why I pushed, why I fought . . ."

"What do you mean pushed?"

"I mean, well . . . as of this morning, I not only lost my own job, but my boss was threatening a lawsuit. They told me it was too raw, too controversial . . . so I pushed the deadline until the last minute, then turned it in within seconds before it went to print. By the time they realized, it was too late. The presses were running, and it had gone live on the web."

"You lost your job?"

"Only briefly. That was before it went viral . . . by then, it was too late to take it down. It had gotten picked up by every outlet in town. CNN even called wanting me to be on Wolf's *The Situation Room.* My boss changed his tune pretty quickly. So, this time, it worked out."

"But what if it didn't? Seriously, Blake . . . why would you take that kind of risk?"

"C'mon, Olivia!" he says, suddenly frustrated. He paces back and forth, running his hand through his already messy hair. "Seriously, you're one of the smartest women I've ever . . . I mean, it makes no sense. Why can't you get this?"

It's unnerving, seeing Blake like this—Blake, who always knows what to say, Blake, who never loses his journalistic distance, his aloof cool. Yet suddenly, here he is, shaking his head and ranting. Stumbling over his words. He stops suddenly and stares at her.

"You lost everything, and so did I. We both built our lives back—not the same lives we'd had, but lives. But it changes you, falling that far. You don't believe in the stuff you once did. That people are genuine, that they care. But you . . . you fell harder than I did, harder than most people could ever imagine . . . and you were right there, giving everything that you had to that job. He shakes his head. "What that girl did to you, well . . . I wasn't going to let it happen again. You deserved redemption. That's why I did it."

Olivia laughs, shocked. "Oh, I see," she says, touched. "Is that all?"

"One other thing," he says matter-of-factly. "I'm in love with you. So, there's that too."

In all the words she's ever learned, all the ones she's ever spoken . . . in a lifetime of words, she'd never find the right follow-up words to that. So, Olivia makes the smart choice—she doesn't speak. She takes a few steps forward, lifts his chin, and smiles . . . and kisses him instead.

Epilogue

Six Months Later

Olivia finally got her own place. True, it isn't that much bigger than her bedroom in New Jersey—the landlord says 900 square feet, but she's pretty sure he's counting the outdoor hallway she shares with her neighbor. That doesn't matter. It's got a bedroom for Gwynnie, and the living room that doubles as one for her. "If you don't like it, you can stay in New Jersey," she'd told her daughter when first giving her a tour. "I mean, I'll stay at Grandma's house a few nights a week, then you can come here on weekends and you . . ."

"Are you kidding, Mom?" Gwynnie asked "No way I'm staying in Jersey . . . this is the coolest, most bohemian shit I've ever seen!"

Olivia had tried to stay neutral, but secretly, she'd been thrilled. Gwynnie didn't mind the commute back from school, either. Just an excuse to put off homework. "I can always cram on the train ride." The homework was just a show—spring semester of her senior year, and she already had acceptances to several schools. Her top choice, the arts school at VCU, had even thrown in a full scholarship.

"What if I come back like one of those uptight, know-it-all liberal arts girls?" She'd said a few nights earlier over takeout Thai. "You know, all faux-artistic types, spouting uninformed PC bullshit and pretending to be woke."

"Never would happen," Olivia had said, mouth full of Larb Gai. "You couldn't be anything but Gwynnie, not even if you tried."

"True," said Gwynnie. "And why would I? I don't have to pretend at anything. I've been woke since the day I was born."

Across the table, Blake had laughed.

"What's so funny?" Asked Gwynnie. "Just wait till I major in creative writing, then you'll see. I know you're, like, having a moment . . . but just wait. I'll give you a run for your money, mark my words."

"I'd put money on it," he'd said.

Gwynnie had grinned. "So, you gonna eat that spring roll or what?"

***

Gwynnie teased Blake mercilessly, but she was as proud of him as Olivia, her Mom. Ever since the Harper

James article, he'd been in hot demand. He'd even gotten a job offer from a big corporate entity—the one that had frozen him out of the journalism world years earlier. He could write about anything he wanted, they'd insisted, and the idea had been intriguing. "I could cover politics again," he'd mused to Olivia. But as of yet, he hadn't taken the leap. "Maybe one day," he'd said. "But for now, I'm gonna stick to this fashion thing."

Some things, some people Olivia had come to understand, just seem to fit. Once you found them, it was so right . . . even if you had the right words, there was no need to describe. It was enough to know they existed, were always with each other on some level, even when apart. That they were there, pulsing with your every heartbeat.

Blake was like that. He still had his own studio downtown, and they weren't attached at the hip . . . but they saw each other plenty. He slept over several nights a week and ate breakfast with Gwynnie before school. *Hey, bro*, she'd greet him in the morning, with a familiarity that made Olivia smile. It wasn't *hey dad*, but from the way she said it . . . it was almost like she was testing the waters, and maybe one day would upgrade.

They'd move in together one day, Olivia and Blake, that seemed destined. Buy a place of their own, rent a cabin in Hawaii, write a book, get married . . . they discussed everything they planned on doing, and it would happen with time. But the when wasn't as important; finding each other was enough for now.

***

Olivia had seen it, of course. But even now, it didn't quite feel real.

The space wasn't large, but the location was everything. Right on 5th Avenue—a few blocks from Harper James, ironically—in fashion's main artery. Sandwiched between an up-and-coming French designer and high-end boutique, the place was perfect, but the rent unfathomable. In the end, Jasmin had put her foot down. *You're taking it, she'd* explained on FaceTime from Dubai. *You have no choice. I'm the one investing the money, so I get the final word.*

I thought it was your husband's money, Olivia had teased.

Shut up, sweetie. Ultimately, who gives a flip where the cash comes from? It was my idea, that's what matters. I'm the visionary who knows talent when I see it. She grinned and pointed directly at the camera. *Yes, I'm talking about you.*

Jasmin had reached out the day after the WSD article came out. For the first minute of the call, she only got out five words. *It's Jasmin. I read it.* The rest of the time had been an endless cascade of uncontrollable laughter. When she'd finally gotten herself together, she offered a real congratulations. *It took someone like you, Olivia. To finally call those 5th Avenue bitches out. Fucking coo-coo couture crazytown.* After that, she got straight to business—her styling work had taken off in Dubai, her schedule packed. Her clients still went on shopping excursions to New York, though, and were left without a stylist they could trust. "So, I think you should be their go-to," Jasmine had explained. "But forget some corporate bullshit. You've met manufacturers, designers—the ones you don't know now you'll find and connect with. Everyone loves you, and with that article, your reputation is even more widespread. So now is the time to capitalize; we've got to jump on this."

Jasmin would invest startup money, covering rent, advertising and other initial costs. She'd take a commission off every sale until Olivia was up and running. Of course, Jasmin's clients would get priority, but they were just the start. "You'll be widely popular, I know it," Jasmin had insisted. You'll be so successful, they'll all be begging to get in. "You'll see, Olivia. This time, it'll be the fashion world curtseying to you."

They opened in a few weeks, and Olivia had a lot left to do. There were the small things—hors-d'oeuvres for the opening day reception, new business announcements to be sent to her growing list of contacts—and the bigger things too. Advertising, for one—Blake had pulled some strings, getting her write ups in several magazines, but was it enough? Even though she'd reached out to every potential client she could think of, placed ads in several publications and told everyone she knew . . . would they care?

At least the place was ready, there was that. The walls had been freshly painted with Benjamin Moore's Chantilly Lace and the polished mahogany floors gleamed. Her own platform, covered in dark navy velvet, set up in the corner. She'd even gotten adjustable lights for the trifold mirror, emulating different times of day.

It had been a lot of work, but she wasn't in it alone. When she'd called Ruby, proposing she leave Harper James for a personal assistant job, the answer had come quick. "I'll pay you well and you can assist in the styling."

"Yes!" Ruby interrupted. "When do I start?"

Ruby had been thrilled. Harper James was bad before, she'd explained. "But ever since that article, it's been a horror movie. So much has happened, Olivia . . ."

Olivia wanted to shut down the conversation that instant. She'd done everything she could to distance herself from that place, afraid even thinking about it would suck her into some painful mental vortex. But as Ruby continued, filling her in on various fates, she couldn't bring herself to say stop.

Part of her wanted to know. Needed to know.

Some of the information she was already aware of—Marcus's fate, for instance. Soon after the article came out, Marcus had beat them to the punch, offering his resignation before he was given no choice. There was no argument, no fuss. He had been quickly identified as the man in the video, and his family had stepped in, Olivia surmised, halting him before any further damage might be done to their legacy. At least, that's what she gathered from the write-up on Page Six—the one claiming he was taking a *mental health retreat*. The kind that happens on high-priced, secluded west coast locales involving twelve steps, at the very least.

He was at Rancho Recuperacion; that was the speculation online. One of the most exclusive facilities available, rumored to have most recently housed Kanye West and Lindsay Lohan at the same time. Olivia had pictured him at group therapy, discussing his rock-bottom moment with tears in his eyes. What would he say? *So, this leaked security footage of an underling giving me a BJ, well . . . it kinda went viral. Like, the 50 million hits kind. That was the last count, at least. I'm completely humiliated!*

Or maybe it was all a rumor; maybe Marcus was fine. Guys like him always have a way of bouncing back. They were like roaches, those Masters of the Universe—come the apocalypse, they'd pick themselves up and move along, scurrying through the death and destruction on their million legs, utterly unscathed.

Ruby had gone on to say management was in chaos. With Marcus leaving, the power struggle had reached Game of Thrones worthy levels. "I guess they can't find a replacement COO," Ruby had mused. "But they better hurry, cause this place is more and more fucked with each passing day."

Olivia had given all the right responses—"Really? I had no idea,"—never letting on there was more to that story. In fact, they had found a replacement, but he had turned them down.

"Why would I go back there? I've never been happier in my life, Olivia," Felix had told her when she'd finally reached out to him. "All those years at Harper James, I'd forgotten anything else existed. Now I realize how many things I would like to do. Travel, for example. Did you know there's a tea tour of China? Yes, a thing like that exists, and it is only one option on my very long bucket list."

Olivia had told Felix how happy she was for him; after filling him in on developments in her life, he returned the sentiment. He promised to be at her launch party. Before they said goodbye, she had finally gotten the nerve.

"Felix, I have to say . . . thank you. I know why you left Harpers, and I can't tell you how much it means to me."

"Unnecessary, Olivia. I could say the same for you. Had you not shown up, I would have given up on that place. But you reminded me truly why I once loved it. I would have left at some point, but I am glad I remembered before I did. That's what I'll hold onto the tightest—to what I loved most about my job. As for the rest, well . . . life goes on, I suppose."

It sure does.

Finally, Ruby had arrived at a subject that filled Olivia with both curiosity and fear: The Salon girls. The Salon hadn't been disbanded; if anything, the article had given it a new life. Appointments came in a flood . . . only problem? There was no staff to fill them.

The C-Cups had been let go under a dark cloud, threats of prosecution for theft looming. "Everyone was saying it was over for them," Ruby lamented. "I mean, who will hire you after that? Stealing, snorting coke with clients . . . what kind of work could you be trusted to do?"

The answer was the girl you'd snorted coke with, and the job was publicity. Amby hadn't been upset by the media outing her; if anything, it was good for her career. She'd already been cast as a coke-snorting former tween star in the upcoming Lars Van Trier film. No company would insure her as an actress, but Lars didn't care. *She has authenticity*, he was quoted saying in *Entertainment Weekly*. *The character is broken, haggard, destroyed by the industry and life. Amber is ideal for the role.*

Amby couldn't have been more thrilled.

By the end of the week, both C's had officially joined the pop star's team. They even had titles: Junior Social Media Coordinator and Lead Cross Platform Media Integrator. Olivia's take? They spent their days alternating between posting Amby selfies on Instagram, scoring her drugs and feeding her ego.

Strangely enough, they might have stumbled into their true-life path; the destiny they were always meant to have.

Ursula hadn't been so lucky. Fearing a lawsuit over hijacked store footwear, she'd hightailed it out of town. According to Ruby, she'd gone home to her family.

"Where are they from?" Olivia had asked, the possibilities running through her head. *Germany, Istanbul? Norway, France? Maybe the Italian countryside, or a picturesque Greek Island.*

"West Virginia," Ruby had said. "Though nobody knows exactly what part."

Only one left to go . . . Olivia had sucked in her breath, waiting to hear the name.

"So, I guess that's about it," Ruby had finished. "Seriously, what a mess. They are trying to re-staff the Salon, and I know I could put in my name, but . . . that place has bad mojo, I feel it. I need a fresh start and . . . voila! You called! I'm so lucky, Olivia. I owe you everything! I'll be the best assistant ever, and you have no idea how glad I am to get out of this place."

She never thought to mention Zoe. She wasn't at the Salon; Felix said she was immediately let go. But where? After the call, Olivia had scoured the web. Beyond references to Blake's article—she'd been quickly identified and been nicknamed BJ Bobblehead on message boards—there was nothing else.

It was as though she'd become invisible. And that, Olivia decided, was just right.

Of course, there was one other person who hadn't been mentioned, but Olivia was well aware of her fate.

She had her on speed dial, in fact, and called her several times a day.

"Marguerite."

Anytime Olivia had a question, which was constantly, Marguerite was the first to call. And when her new store was nearing completion, of course Marguerite was the first person she invited on a tour.

Olivia had been more nervous than she expected, letting loose with an unexpected stream of babbling. *It isn't quite ready yet, you know, but maybe you'll get an idea how it . . . well, I mean, it's almost ready, but there are some elements missing. Nothing big, but once I get the fixtures in place and the window treatments installed . . .*

"Olivia!" Marguerite had barked, stopping her cold. "You sound frantic!"

"I am frantic!"

"Here is the only thing you need to know, Olivia. It will be lovely. A huge success. You took a risk, and it will pay off in perfection. So, stop with the worrying—and the babbling, I implore you!—there's no need." She nodded, smiling with certainty. "Everything will turn out more wonderful than you could have ever possibly imagined in your wildest dreams."

"Guess I could say the same about you," Olivia had said, glancing down at her finger. "Wow! I still can't get over the size of that rock! Who knew Willard had such great taste?"

"Well, he might have had some subtle guidance," Marguerite had said, practically glowing. "But I will say one thing—I feel like the luckiest woman alive."

***

The day before her official opening, Olivia circled the shop, going through her checklist one last time. Everything seemed to be in place, from the bursting stockroom in back—networking with designers and manufacturers had paid off, and Jasmin was right, the ones she didn't know were more than thrilled to meet her—to the gleaming shop windows in front. The vinyl window decals had come that day, so it was finally official to the world at large: *Olivia Kopelman* in elegant black cursive on the glass, and the words *Private Client Styling* underneath.

The official opening would be tomorrow at 7:00 p.m., for her soft launch party. She was ready for that too. The flowers had been delivered, the smell of lilies permeating the room; the menu had been set and the caterers scheduled to arrive at 5:00 p.m. Brochures were printed and her new business cards already in their case. The RSVPs had all arrived, the majority marked yes, so now there was nothing left to do but close her eyes and imagine it going off perfectly.

Olivia does just that. She leans against the wall, engulfed in the scent of fresh flowers, and pictures what is to come. Not just the party, but the day after that, and the ones to follow. In that instant, she knows. *Marguerite was right.*

Everything will turn out more wonderfully than Olivia could have possibly imagined. She puckers, applies french tulip shimmer and relishes in her feeling of authentic happiness. She can't even remember the last time she was this elated.

***

With 45 minutes to go until showtime, Olivia realized there was someone she just had to talk to . . . just even for a minute. Olivia's biggest cheerleader (well, except Gladys and Gwynnie of course.) "Hello?" answered a woman with a voice that warmed Olivia's heart and made her feel right at home. "Daphne! Oh my God . . . I am so happy you answered! You just won't believe what has happened." Olivia, so excited to finally connect with her very dear friend. "Oh, Olivia! How wonderful to hear from you! I miss you so much! Anyway, no time for unnecessary pleasantries. You know how much I adore you. Now, tell me everything."

About the Author

Toni Glickman is a former retail executive, who spent twenty years in the cashmere and silk-studded front lines in the luxury space of this piranha infested industry. Toni, in her provocative new book *Bitches of Fifth Avenue,* reveals the story of life behind the luxury lines—what the client never sees. The exhaustion, depression, and anxiety-ridden days of an employee's experience, which clients never realize. The fear of low sales numbers, of losing rank, of losing a job to someone with a better client book. Also, there's the fear of returned merchandise and the constant worry of losing a client to another salesperson. Never a moment of purity, or peace, or calm. It is a life lived constantly on the edge. *Saks Fifth Avenue*, *Prada*, *Jil Sander*, *Chanel*, *Bloomingdale's* and *Burberry*—these were just a few brands in which Toni achieved success before ultimately being backstabbed by those she thought she could trust.

Moving up the ladder from sales associate to industry executive, Toni Glickman compares working in the field to the front lines of a minefield. Her colleagues exemplified the mines which she had to navigate through in order to survive and make her sales numbers, which is all that matters at the end of the day when the cash registers close. An employee in this industry is only respected by how much business is done, in business lingo: "day over day, month over month, and year over year." Expectations run high, illness is not permitted, and personal lives are ignored. It is report after report, endless conference calls, sales strategies, and goals. Personal shoppers do whatever it takes—it is sell, sell, sell.

Toni Glickman now enjoys life as a real estate professional, where she sets her own schedule and no longer needs to contend with maneuvering "bitchy" retail colleagues. She's also a Francophile, plays classical piano, loves the cinema, travel, her children, family, friends, and Teacup Pomeranian.

Now Available!

TONI GLICKMAN
BITCHES OF FIFTH AVENUE
BOOK ONE – BOOK TWO

For more information
visit: www.SpeakingVolumes.us

Now Available!

JORDAN S. KELLER
ASHES OVER AVALON TRILOGY

**For more information
visit:** www.SpeakingVolumes.us

Now Available!

STACY LEE
PRICKLY PEN INVESTIGATIONS
BOOK ONE

**For more information
visit:** <www.SpeakingVolumes.us>

Now Available!

CHARLENE WEXLER
MURDER ON SKID ROW

**For more information
visit: www.SpeakingVolumes.us**

www.ingramcontent.com/pod-product-compliance
Lightning Source LLC
LaVergne TN
LVHW041704070526
838199LV00045B/1190